M000032003

ARCH RECRUIT

CHAD LOWREY

NOTEBOOK PUBLISHING

First published in 2020 by Notebook Publishing of
Notebook Group Limited, 20–22 Wenlock Road,
London, N1 7GU.

www.notebookpublishing.co

ISBN: 9781913206611

A CIP catalogue record for this book is available
from the British Library.

Typeset by Notebook Publishing.

CHAPTER 1

"I need you guys to focus on our target and quit playing grab ass out there, got it? Ali Iman Salweem is the only guy we're concerned with right now. You've all been given a picture of him so he can be positively identified. Keep collateral damage to an absolute minimum. You'll more than likely see some fight back. We need a quick take on this one. He's going to have a handful or two of his goons by him at all times; that means we need to observe and take when the picking is right. Watch for civilians and human shields because we know these jackasses like to play that game. Bottom line, boys, we need him alive. Any questions?"

There were five pairs of highly trained eyes on me at this moment; each of these guys hand-picked and trained to the tune of a couple million dollars each. The foreplay of the mission was complete. It was time to dip the wick. Each special operations mission is like a Broadway show: you have to rehearse in order to bring the house down. If something didn't go as planned we were trained to adapt and, at times, improvise, but we always overcame. This team had been together for the better part of a year and we had yet to lose a team member. Some people said we were too stubborn to die.

The team consisted of Staff Sergeant Marcus Stewart, Sergeant Jimmy Witherspoon, Sergeant James Andrews, Lieutenant Mark Wood, Staff Sergeant Bob Kimber, and myself, Captain Orion Thorrsen—or more affectionately known as Stew, Spooner, Doc, Wood, Shooter McGavin, and Thor, respectively. All of the men were cross-trained and knew one another's job on the team.

Stew was our weapons guy. Spooner was our engineer; the one we called on when we needed to blow shit up. Doc was our medic. Wood was our intelligence guy. Shooter McGavin was in charge of comms or communications; he got his nickname from being an absolutely shitty golfer, and though he claimed to love the game he couldn't hit water if he fell out of a boat. I was the OIC or Officer in Charge. Having the last name of Thorrsen, I was given the nickname Thor relatively early in life.

Stew and I had served together for six years and had become more brothers than two people could be if there were born to the same mom. He was a twenty-eight year old black man from Philly who had joined the Army as a way out of the downward spiral that lay before him in the streets. He was a human version of a Pitbull: he was nice as could be, but piss him off and he would go for blood. He had two modes: 'I don't care' and 'kill'.

Spooner was an American-born Filipino who had joined because he wanted to defend the U.S. against all enemies, foreign and domestic, following 9/11. He was a twenty-four year old former high school wrestler who was as patriotic as they come.

Doc grew up back east and had a wicked cool accent. He was twenty-four as well, and the only bad thing about Doc was that he was a Patriots and Tom Brady fan.

Wood was from South Carolina and had grown up on a farm out there. His family raised hogs and he used to do a lot of that obstacle course racing, Tough Mudder, Spartan Race shit. He could run circles around all of us, even at thirty-eight years old.

Shooter McGavin was twenty-six and grew up somewhere in California. If you slapped a bleached blond wig on him, he'd complete the whole surfer look that his accent carried with it.

I was the second oldest of the bunch at thirty-six. I grew up in Utah, playing football and baseball in high school. I had started college and slid through getting a bullshit degree majoring in billiards and Sociology.

There wasn't a whole lot of idle chit chat as we exited the crumbling brick building that was our center of operations. The team's focus was intense; we were ready for the fight that was about to go down. The rotors of the helicopter loudly drummed our theme song. We each sat in the webbing that lined the sides of the bird and strapped in.

"Hey, Thor, if this guy is anything like our last Uber driver, I'm only giving him three stars." Stew was always the one to help lighten the mood.

"Stew, it's not our fault the bartender cut you off and made us leave the bar. Not to mention that when the Uber driver *did* get there, you tried asking about the picture of his hot sister that he had on the dash only to find out it was his wife," I clapped back.

The other guys chuckled at the retort. Most of them were there that night and had either witnessed the events or heard about it when the second Uber got back to my place. "Not only that, when you *did* find out it was his wife, it probably wasn't the smart play to ask 'So, does that mean you're not going to give me her number?'. You're lucky you're built like a brick shithouse, Stew."

Even Stew was laughing now. With a flip of his hand and sarcastic *pshh*, he waved me off and we all laid our heads back to focus or catch a quick nap before we unleashed Armageddon on some unsuspecting asshat who had orchestrated the bombings of an outpost three months before, taking the lives of two American Marines.

The flight crew ran through their checks and the CH47 Chinook helicopter lifted off the ground, kicking up the dust. The night quickly enveloped us as we started towards the small mountain village in the mountains of Afghanistan. There was a special kind of peace that you feel surging through the air in the middle of the night—even in the loud, steel-skinned "shithook". Almost an hour had passed since we'd taken off and I hadn't slept a minute of it. I unbuckled my straps and began checking the guys' equipment. We had all checked each other several times to make sure we had the necessary items, but when you're in the military you gain a special form of OCD. If you didn't have OCD before joining the military, you did after. It's like that shit comes as standard issue. If, on the other hand, you had OCD before joining, well shit, then you were like a squirrel on meth-laced crack. In this case, you learn to check, recheck, triple-check and double-triple check yourself *and* each other before and after each mission. Every piece of equipment had a place in your ruck or on your person, or some other method of being carried with you. The last thing you wanted was to be searching for a magazine or another vital item when the enemy was trying to turn you into a lead sponge. After checking each member of the team, I smacked their shoulder in approval and moved on to the next.

The bird had started to descend and the flight crew was gathering the ropes and preparing for us to repel down. The pilot had lowered us to seventy-five feet above the ground as the crew threw the ropes out the tail end. We all stood up, and as I walked to the back of the Chinook, I looked each and every member in the eyes. Not a word was said, but each one of us knew.

Wood and Doc slid down the ropes first. Spooner and Stew were next, then Shooter and myself. The nylon rope warmed my gloved hands as I quickly slid down. My boots gently thudded on the dirt below. Looking up to the crew above, I signaled that we were all good before they took off to wait just outside of the target area. Quickly and quietly, we set up our perimeter. We were a well-oiled machine. I took a brief moment to admire the fluidity of the team; I was like a proud father watching his children stand at the plate down by one with two outs. We were going to knock this mission out of the park.

The small collection of mud huts and shacks two-hundred yards in front of us looked as if a yard full of twelve year old kids had been instructed to build a bunch of clubhouses. They were shanties at best. It was hard to believe that the "assistant to the regional manager" of the terrorist faction trusted this place with his life planning his attacks sitting on old wooden crates and dirt floors. In addition to the recent bombing, he orchestrated multiple suicide bombings at checkpoints across the region and attacks on local army installations. On a scale of zero and piece of shit, he was a steaming pile.

The dark blanket of moonless night provided the perfect cover as we crept toward the target house. We scattered to our predetermined positions and covered one another as we leapfrogged from small tree, rock or shanty until we were twenty yards from the four walls and corrugated roof that held our HVT—high value target. With the exception of the one guard outside and his sleeping counterpart, there were no obstacles into the adobe vault.

The roaming guard was eighteen years old at best. Most of the men this group had "recruited" were sixteen or just over. Some had seen a few years of skirmishes and somehow had lived to see their early twenties, but the median age of the group was twenty-one. For being so young, they had quite the terroristic resume. Salweem was twenty-eight and had known nothing but the Middle East thug life. He was kidnapped at twelve years old, but over the years had proven himself loyal to the cause. After all, ranking members above him had moved up due to the open positions made possible by 'Merica and our allied countries', Salweem himself was granted the position he would hold for about another fifteen minutes.

All eyes trained on me. Without speaking a word, the positions were relayed to each member via orchestrated hand signals. On my final signal, we quietly sprang into action. Spooner threw a rock behind the roaming guard as a diversion, and once the unsuspecting kid turned around, readying his weapon, Wood leapt behind him, kicking the back of his knees to buckle him down. After falling to his knees, Wood slammed the butt of his weapon into the back of the young kid's head. He Vanilla Iced him and, in no time at all, he was out cold. The sleeping sentry was roused by the slight sound of his partner being knocked out, and before he could stand up, he was kissed by the butt end of Wood's rifle.

Two for two. Nobody had to die unless they *had* to die.

The team lined up, hugging the wall outside the front door. Counting down from three on his fingers, Stew, the lead man, signaled for us to go in. There were two other guys on the floor next to Salweem who lay next to two girls. The girls were young, maybe in their twenties.

All in all the capture was uneventful. The two men woke up to rifles being hard pressed into their cheeks, just below their eyes, by Stew and Shooter. Spooner and Doc kept the girls in check, and I had our target, Ali Iman Salweem; his hands zip-tied behind his back and mouth taped within a minute and a half. If this were a human rodeo, we would have won the buckle for terrorist roping.

After a few minutes of quieting the other two guys and the two girls, we began to move them outside. We would have to make it two-hundred yards without being detected with our cache of hostages. "Alright, boys, Shooter called for the Uber; it'll be here in fifteen minutes. We need to keep them quiet and get them all to the pick-up spot. You know the plan, let's move."

In a practiced, orderly fashion, we led Salweem and his entourage to the door of the hut.

One of the girls tripped over Spooner's boot as we lined them up, and she fell forward to the ground. Given the close quarters, Spooner wasn't able to get hands on her immediately and she scrambled through the legs of Wood and Shooter before launching herself out the door.

"Shit! Thor, she's outside!" Spooner yelled out and immediately tried making his way through the doorway to get her back. The second that young lady's lungs hit outside air, they gave way to a screaming siren of alarm.

"MOVE!" I clenched on to the back of Salweem's robes and forced him out as we followed the team forward. We would have to book it to the landing zone and forget about the escapee. She had given us away, and our only chance was to get out, get to the LZ, and take cover until our ride showed up.

Running with our other hostages, we darted in between shanties and rickety outhouses. On the outskirts of the village, with thirty yards left to go before we could take cover behind the scant trees and plentiful rocks, all hell broke loose.

I heard garbled yelling, and then I heard the *pop*. In front of me I saw the bullet tear through Stew's left thigh. "Contact left! Return fire!" I commanded. I shoved Salweem forward onto the ground by Doc and yelled for him, Spooner and Shooter to take him and the rest to the edge of the houses. Wood and I would give cover fire and get Stew to safety. A lone gunman had positioned himself on a rooftop about a hundred yards away and was trying to finish Stewart off. Wood and I had found refuge behind the burned out carcass of what used to be a car and continued giving cover fire while Stew lay barren on the dirt twenty yards in front of us. He was thrown down by the shot and landed with a thud. The weight of him and his equipment, in addition to his momentum, threw him forward, face first into the unforgiving dirt and rocky earth. He was exposed out in the open, vulnerably waiting for his turn to absorb more fire from our enemy. Hunkering behind the car while Wood covered Stew, I threw off my gear and readied myself to grab Stewart.

The Army teaches you the Warrior's Ethos in basic training. It's driven into your head so that the words are more than just a repeated phrase. The Drill Sergeants screaming in your face, forcing you to repeat the ethos as you stand at attention, doesn't only force your mind to remember it, but your whole body to absorb it. It becomes a belief, a way of conducing yourself. It becomes who you are. The four sentences of the ethos empower you to believe in yourself.

"I will always place the mission first."

"I will never accept defeat."

"I will never quit."

"I will never leave a fallen comrade."

From Day One of Basic Training, you hear these words over and over and over. There are posters throughout your barracks, the chowhall, in every classroom. They give you a laminated card to keep in your shoulder pocket, and it becomes an inspectable piece of equipment. You're ordered to keep it on your person at all times. On the final day of Basic Training, the four sentences become your battle cry. Throughout your Army career, you subconsciously apply them to every single situation you face in life. Whether you are at the club or capturing High Value Targets, no comrade will be left behind. That's because you have placed the mission first. Because you won't accept defeat and you absolutely won't quit.

The sniper had been joined by two others as the hard, packed earth around Stewart and the car that Wood and I hid behind spit dirt upwards from the shots being fired.

"Marcus?! You alright? Hold on, I'm coming to get you!" I could hear the grunts of pain over the gunfire. Peeking around the ass end of the car, I could see him trying to steady his rifle and pop some shots at the snipers who wanted nothing more than to take him out. "Ry, don't you dare! I'm pinned down. They'll pick you off!"

The three gunmen were now five. There were like moths to a flame. The rounds flew through the air like mosquitos at a barbecue. It was the impossible nightmare. Meanwhile, Doc had helped get the remaining captured to the LZ and made his way back to help fend off the amassing force.

There are times when you have an impending feeling of death and it appears as if there is no way out of your situation. This was one of those times. I knew without really stopping to analyze anything that if we didn't hurry the hell up and find a way out of this fuster cluck of a situation—and quickly—we'd all end up staring at the roof of a church. Yelling over the pop-shot chaos, I asked Doc if the Chinook had made it to pick us up.

"No, they're not there yet! Shooter tried to call in a hurry-up and also get us some air established back-up, but the office said they were out for the night and to call back after 0600!" The grin on his face and the maniacal laugh masked his fear.

We often make jokes during such situations, subconsciously deflecting our true feelings. But Doc wasn't wired that way; it wasn't in his DNA to feel fear. Doc was a battle-tested man who had seen five deployments during his time in Spec Ops. The message I'm sure Doc had received was that there were no available forces to back us up. Apparently there was another group of elite soldiers that were pinned down and needed air support elsewhere—at least, that's what I told myself.

As Wood was popping off rounds, he had apparently taken one of the snipers out and immediately yelled out, "Winner, winner!" before immediately going back to covering Stewart.

With all of my extra gear off and only wearing my Kevlar helmet and IOTV (Improvised Outer Tactical Vest; a.k.a. bullet proof vest), I shouted for Wood and Doc to cover me while I went to get Stewart in an effort to get him out of the shooting barrel. I had to rush the twenty yards between Stew and I, pick him up, and bring him to safety without getting tagged by those shitty shooting asshats who were dead set on ruining our extraction party.

Those twenty yards may as well have been two-hundred. I knew that, instead of dodging bullets, I was more likely to absorb one or two. But I also knew that it didn't matter. It was never a question. I would never leave a fallen comrade, especially a man I considered my brother. "I'm going out! Get my six!"

The other two ramped up their return fire as I leapt out from the security of the metal carcass and into the open. The gunfire was deafening, yet still I could hear the screams and hollers of my guys as they gave the enemy a fearful war cry. I could feel the heat from the bullets as they buzzed through the air, skimming past my head. The smell of carbon from the fight was stifling. As I dove around the car wreck and hurdled the debris in the dirt street, the world around me somehow muffled and time seemed to slow. I could hear my own heartbeat. *Boom-BOOM... Boom-BOOM... Boom-BOOM...* It was as if I had jumped into the deep end of a pool and all I could hear was the stifled screams of the people around me.

The pressure in the air, the compression of sound, the feeling of claustrophobia had numbed the reality of death that sailed all around me. Sergeant Stewart's thigh looked like an exploded hot dog. The bullet had torn through the upper portion of his thigh after entering from the back.

Marcus Stewart was not just another soldier; he was my brother in arms. He'd saved my life a year earlier, during a previous deployment when, as we'd searched door-to-door for a suspected cache of weapons, we'd entered what we thought was an abandoned home. I was point man and the first to enter after Sparta-kicking the front door open. I hadn't seen the man with the gun hiding in the rafters as we rushed in. Stewart was second man and entered immediately after me. I cleared the room and the corners, but it was Sgt. Stewart who saw the predator waiting above us. Stewart shoved me down to the ground and took him out with one shot. I owed him a debt. We'd grown up in similar scenarios but on opposite ends of the states. He was in Philadelphia, and I bounced from California to Utah. He'd grown up in the system and in one of the hardest places to survive in the eastern states. I, at least, didn't have that card in the hand I'd been dealt, but we both had the deck stacked against us. Somehow, we'd both come out on top.

Out of debt and brotherhood, even if I didn't manage to reach him in time and we both met our fates on this dirt floor hell, I had to try to save him. It was a moral imperative.

I reached Marcus with a few more leaps and immediately began packing the wound and placing a tourniquet on his leg above the mess of tissue. I had to control the bleeding or else my whole Matrix-like bullets-dodging display would be for nothing.

"Thor, I can't walk. My leg looks like SpongeBob's ass!" He was yelling over the roar of the firefight. His breathing was labored, and he'd lost quite a bit of blood already. From the looks of it, his femoral artery had been severed. My hope was that the tourniquet would hold long enough for him to make it to surgery or, at the very least, the next echelon of care. He would be staged in a Forward Operating Base, before being given a medivac to Landstuhl, Germany. Any more wasted time and Marcus's story would be told in an obituary.

"Marcus, I'm getting you out of here. Give me your arm." With every ounce of strength I could muster, I hooked his arm over my shoulders and hoisted his six-foot, two-hundred and twenty-pound frame over me to carry him out fireman's style. The movement must have sent searing pain through his leg as he screamed out when I began to lift.

"Dammit, Thor, if you're trying to kill me, those jackasses on the rooftop beat you to it!"

I could feel his body tense from the pain. His attempt at humor brought a forced laugh to my throat. His left leg—the bleeding of which had started to slow yet continued to paint the front of me—hung limp against my chest as I began to trudge the twenty yards back to cover. I could feel the warmth of his exposed flesh and blood as it stained my uniform. The reality of our surroundings became clearer as the bullets pierced the air and dove angrily into the ground around us.

I'd taken only five steps when I saw the light. It was still midnight-dark outside and couldn't have been more than two-thirty in the morning, local time. The light wasn't bright, but rather like a hot stretch of road on a summer day. The air in front of me gave way to the waves of barely visible light. I immediately noticed it in front of me as it grew brighter, grew taller, piercing the darkness of night.

Two more trudging steps.

It had now fully encompassed me and Sgt. Stewart. At first, I thought it was my body reacting to the weight of Stewart by throwing flashing stars into my vision, but as I moved forward I could make out fine details in the air. I could see the waves of faint light as they began to take shape. I saw the small tips of what appeared to be feathers as they morphed into full wings. They were coming from behind us and seemed to be wrapping themselves around the two of us. The edges of the wings and every detail were visible, but I could see through them like a cheap, white hotel curtain. I looked to my left and then to my right, searching for cover or some form of protection. I could see the wings take full form all around us. It was then that I felt the presence of hands pushing me from the back. These were no dainty, valentine cherub hands. They were the strong, powerful hands of a full grown man.

Five more lumbering steps.

I could hear the enemy's gunfire all around us, but felt nothing. I looked back to the rooftop to one of the snipers. Our eyes met, and he slowly raised his weapon to his shoulder and readied it to fire. His lips moved as he mumbled something. I saw his finger as it gently hugged the trigger and then I saw the muzzle flash.

Time slowed to a crawl. I watched the bullet dance through the air as it surged towards my head. I saw Diesel, the Great Dane I'd had when I was eight years old; the summer that he and I spent every day at the reservoir. I saw the stadium with stands full of people as I caught Johnny Larson's pass and ran for a touchdown, winning the state championship my Junior year. I saw my Senior Prom; Lori Clark my date and a group of friends in tow. We'd rented a limo and played out the first of many 'nights of our lives'. I saw the enlistment room at the Army recruiting station the day I raised my right hand and swore to defend the constitution of the United States against all enemies foreign and domestic.

I was helpless as I watched the beautiful spiral of the metal pierce the air ten feet from my face. A brilliant flash of light erupted immediately in front of me, exactly where the bullet should have buried itself in my skull. The light seemed to vibrate the air around me, making small rippling waves in the light-edged wings that still surrounded us. The fragmented bullet fell to the ground. I had taken five more steps.

The sounds of battle had begun to resurge, and I could hear and see everything around me. The wings, along with the bright light outlining them, had vanished. The veiled surroundings, hidden by their fullness, had since been restored. The violent pop of the M4 rifles of Doc and Wood continued their coverage of me and Marcus as I lumbered the last ten feet to cover. Three other insurgents were taken out by the cover fire while I carried Sgt. Stewart to safety.

Marcus's body fell heavily to the ground and went rigid from the pain of movement. His scream filled the dusty, chaotic war-torn air and his profanity-laced tirade let me know that he at least still had feeling in his leg, which gave me a little bit of reassurance. The final sniper was felled with a well-placed shot from Doc Andrews. We could hear the distant thud of the Chinook blades as they chopped through the mountain air.

The big, green, metallic angel landed on the hard ground as the crew rushed to Spooner and the hostages. While I gathered my equipment, Doc and Wood had taken their uniform tops off and tied them together in such a way to enable us to lay Marcus on it and hastily drag him across the dirt and small shrubs to our ride out of hell. The flight crew met us halfway with a stretcher. They loaded up Stewart as Wood, Doc, and I continued on. We used most of our First Aid supplies during the fight and while hidden behind the car before making the run to safety.

Spooner had loaded Iman Salweem into the helicopter, and before the rest of us had stepped in, he cut the remaining hostages loose. They fell to the ground as they hurriedly rushed away from American infidel aircraft, while we collapsed from exhaustion on the webbing and the floor of the Chinook.

The angry drumming of the rotors ramping up drowned out the organized chaos within the belly of the bird as it became all hands on deck to help keep Marcus Stewart alive. Hastily lifting off the ground, we began to fly, nose first through the darkness.

The edges of the horizon started to light from the impending dawn that was a little more than a couple hours away. During the flight, I could only hear bits and pieces of the radio calls demanding for medical help to meet us when we landed at our destination. We made an hour flight in just over thirty minutes, thanks to a heavy-footed pilot and a healthy tail wind. We approached the airfield, which was just outside the hospital, as I began to take stock of my crew and our gear. The floor of the bird was a deep, dark red that sloshed in spots. Unbeknownst to me when we loaded up for the escape trip, Wood had a grazing wound to his right shoulder from shrapnel. His right arm hung slightly limp at his side, but he never said one thing, nor did he complain; everyone's concern was with Stewart. He was fading fast, and had now stopped responding. Upon landing, we were rushed by a throng of medics and doctors as they carried, pushed, applied, and poked every piece of medical equipment needed towards, around, onto and into Stew. A few of the medics had turned to the rest of us and began to triage the injuries. Over the confusion, I could hear Wood tell one of the medics, "Get the hell out of my face! Go take care of *him*!", thrusting his dirtied, gloved finger in Stewart's direction.

After being stabilized, Stewart was transferred to Germany for surgery to repair his leg. The gunshot had shattered his femur and taken a fist-sized chunk of flesh from his thigh.

Wood, in his words, was "given a fucking bandaid. It was a flesh wound, Thor. Quit worrying about it". He was the most hard-charging, bad ass medic I ever had the honor of working with. Spooner and Doc were given a thirty-two point checkup and took a couple of bags of saline by IV to help with dehydration. They tried giving me a once-over, looking for any unknown or hidden injuries. I just pushed them away and kept my silent vigil for Stewart. He would end up having two surgeries at Landstuhl before doctors thought him stable enough to transfer stateside.

That was the last time our team would go on a mission, overcome, adapt and improvise together.

CHAPTER 2

After our mission, the team was sent back to the States. Doc ended up attending AMEDD, Army Medical Department Center and School, in San Antonio, Texas. He was accepted into the doctorate's program and would graduate at the top of his class, continuing a valiant career saving lives.

Wood was promoted to Team Leader and was given his own group of five rag-tags to babysit, train and save the world with. The last I heard, he was somewhere in the Middle East taking care of what remained of the insurgent cell we had run against.

Spooner apparently had a sister's cousin's friend with some strings to pull, who ended up getting him on with the Secret Service. He was working on the President's personal detail in Washington D.C. and protected him everywhere from the U.S. to Europe as the President and his family traveled the world.

Returning to Ft. Bragg, North Carolina, I started out-processing from the Army immediately after we were debriefed and sent home from the mission. My time in the military had come to a close, and I swore I wouldn't live out my days dodging bullets and growing old being a grunt. The lifestyle was all I had known during my life, and I felt it was time to start anew.

I made it to Headquarters and put in my paperwork for discharge at the same time as putting in paperwork for leave. Before the ink had even dried and well before it even had a chance to be approved, I booked a flight to the Bethesda, Maryland. I was on my way to Walter Reed Army hospital to see Marcus. He was still being treated there in-house due to the severity of his injuries.

Walking into the hospital, I could see every branch of the military represented by personnel wearing their uniforms. Even the puddle-jumpers Coast Guard had people there. Of course, the Chair Force were all over; they had quite a few people stationed there as medical staff, as did the Navy. Now, the Marines had a few people that worked in various positons in the hospital, but not as many as the Navy, Air Force, and Army. I guess they couldn't keep crayons in stock for those glorious, crayon-eating, hard-charging Devil Dog bastards. Given the choice, there is one thing I would always want in a bar fight, and that was a Marine. God loved them and so did I.

I checked in with the hospital information desk and asked for Staff Sergeant Stewart's room. An elderly lady with blue-tinted hair and sweet grandma smile directed me to Room 322, located on the third floor. After exiting the elevator at the right floor, the nurse's station immediately met me as a uniformed woman wearing the rank of Specialist asked what she could do for me. "I'm here to see Staff Sergeant Marcus Stewart. I believe he's in Room 322." The young woman double-checked some papers on the desk and asked me for I.D. After showing her my military identification, she stiffened up to the position of parade rest before I could tell her "at ease". This was respectful military protocol between enlisted personnel and officers.

"Relax, soldier. Relax. You're good."

She softened her stance as she pointed down the hall to where I could find Stew's room.

"Thank you, Specialist. Have a good day".

"Yes, Sir. Thank you," she replied with a smile, and sat back down at the desk. Most of the doors were closed and the hospital staff were coming in and out, going to and from, delivering care to their patients. I quickly arrived at the room and lightly knocked on the heavy wooden door.

"What the problem is?" Stewart called out as I opened the door. "Thor! Holy shit! What's going on, bro? What are you doing here?"

Marcus was lying in bed, his left leg in a traction device to keep it immobilize. His eyes lit up and his grin took over his entire face when he saw me.

Making my way across the room, I stood at his bedside as we embraced in a tight, brotherly hug. I could feel his body jerk from pain, and I immediately backed off. "Ah, shit. I'm sorry, bro."

He waved me off. "This leg gives me pain no matter what I do. Don't worry about it, Thor. It's just certain movements that hurt. That poor excuse for a sniper got off about a hundred rounds and happened to get lucky with one of them." He was humble by nature, but Marcus never bragged about his exploits on any mission. He had saved not only myself time and time again, but the other members of the team on at least one occasion.

Settling back into the bed, he straightened the blankets and reached for the TV's remote control. Judge Joe Brown was ripping into someone's ass on his show. Stewart hit the button and silence fell.

"Hey, sorry to interrupt your stories, man. I can come back later if you want?" I began to laugh as his face twisted in disapproval.

"Man, shut the hell up!" We both laughed at the barbed love. "For real, what are you doing here, Orion?" I could tell he wasn't used to having people visit him. He was far enough away from Philly that any friends or remaining family would have to take a day off of work to make the trip.

"I couldn't let you tell these good people here at the hospital some made-up story about getting shot in the leg. No, Sir. I had to set the story straight and tell them the truth that you were stabbed in the leg by a stripper with a spork from Taco Bell. I tried to tell you, man, you should have paid the woman." I couldn't help but laugh at my own joke, and Marcus joined in but with an added "asshole" and "fuck you". "No, really bro... I couldn't *not* come see you. I didn't even unpack my bags when I got home. I hopped the first flight I could get."

A young woman in an Army uniform knocked and entered. "Sergeant Stewart? Is there anything that I can get for you or your friend?"

This hospital was better than half of the dive hotels I'd ever stayed in. I cleared my throat and asked for some juice if she could round one up for me.

Stewart smiled. "I'm good for now, thank you, Jameson".

The woman's eyes brightened shyly and her cheeks slightly blushed as she embarrassingly looked down, turned around, and closed the door behind her.

"What the hell was that about?" I was confused. She hadn't even acknowledged me or my polite request, but made it clear that the only person in the room was Stew.

"Bro, Sergeant Jameson has been trying to find out 'what's up' since I got here. I guess she's got the fever, man."

I laughed and shook my head. Marcus was a good looking, athletically built black man. I couldn't blame the girl for wanting to know 'what's up'.

We talked for an hour, touching on everything from who had gone to what was new at the Army post and how bad the Philadelphia Eagles were playing this season. I couldn't help but give him grief about his favorite football team. Being a Green Bay fan myself, we rarely had the opportunity for a rivalry game between us, and so I took every chance I could get to rattle him about his team. We caught up on just about everything, but we hadn't talked about that day. Certain things were fair game, but he and I both figured it was over and better left thousands of miles away on those dirt paths—except for one thing: I had to know if Marcus remembered anything about what had happened when I'd carried him out of the firefight. It had bothered me since that day, but I couldn't talk to anybody else about it.

During a small window of silence I decided it was as good a time as any to ask him. "Listen, Stew... There's something I wanted to talk to you about. It's about that day." I looked him in the eyes as he looked down. I could tell he didn't want to go back, but I couldn't let this go. I needed answers. "Stew, when I picked you up and we were taking fire, I saw something. I saw light in front of me and it was blinding, man. I could barely see for a few seconds. It started out really faint but then slowly grew brighter. When I finally could see, I saw an angel... or *something*." I paused. Saying it aloud for the first time, I realized how insane I sounded. I knew it was a man and I knew that I saw wings of some sort, but

I couldn't be a hundred percent sure without hearing that Marcus had seen it, too. I continued on. "It's wings were outstretched in front of us, from behind. They were, they... They were protecting us. They shielded us, the wings did. I saw the rounds coming in at us and they bounced off the... They bounced off the wings, man, or whatever the hell they were. Look, I know it sounds crazy as hell, but I know what I saw. I just need to know if you saw anything, if you remember anything like that..."

I finished and studied his face for any kind of emotion or reaction. His eyes went from the floor to mine, a blank look plastered across his face. He was quiet for what seemed like several minutes. A shade of nervousness washed over him that quickly turned to anger. "Orion, you really gotta lay off the sauce. The only flashes of any light were the muzzles of those guys on the roof. I'm not sure what you saw or what you *think* you saw, but there was no angel soldier or immaculate protection out there. Even after everything that happened, I remember every single second of that day." His voice started to trail off as he tried to rationally explain the muzzle flashes.

I could see something in his eyes that didn't seem right. I'd known Marcus longer than anyone in my military career. I'd seen him drunk, sober, getting ready to "merc" some idiot at the club because the guy tried to shove a girl against the wall.

I even saw him fly from a two-story balcony into the shallow end of a hotel pool in Ft. Lauderdale. I knew more about him than he knew about himself. I could read him like a book—but this time was different. He met my eyes briefly, but immediately looked down at his leg again.

"Look, I'm not crazy. I'm sober and have been since we got back from ass-crack-istan. I... I'm not sure what it was, but there were rounds coming in at us and they missed. I watched as one traced right for me. It was going to hit me square between the eyes, Stew, but they all *missed*, and—"

"Orion, you know those guys can't shoot for shit! They let off hundreds of rounds as I was pinned and I only got hit once directly and absorbed some shrapnel from a few other shots! Once! One hit, Orion! Can you hear yourself right now? Angels, lights... What the hell, man?" His face twisted more, and I could see he was working himself up.

My voice softened and I hung my head, "Look, forget it. Forget I said anything."

We talked for another two hours. We talked about everybody else and almost everything under the sun.

When it was time to leave, I got up and made my way around to his bedside, pushed the tray table aside, and as I did I knocked a small notepad off the table and onto the floor. The pages rolled open as it fell, revealing half-finished drawings. I picked up the book, studying the pages that had fallen open before quickly closing it and setting it back onto the table next to the bed. Marcus acted almost angrily as he reached for the notepad and said, "Just put it on the table. Leave it, it's fine". Emotion seemed to cascade across his face, but he seemed more embarrassed than upset. I nodded, bid him goodbye, and walked out of the room.

I know what I saw that day as Marcus and I dodged the parade of bullets, and I know what I saw in his drawing. I felt the ten-ton weight lift off of my shoulders and I knew, without Marcus telling me, that I wasn't crazy. What I'd seen during our mission and what I'd seen in Marcus's book were the exact same thing; the pencil drawings were quick and some appeared to have been made in haste, but there was a man with large angel-like wings spread forward as one man carried another over his shoulders.

Marcus, I knew, had seen the same light. And he'd seen the same man with huge wings who'd sheltered us from the barrage of gunfire.

CHAPTER 3

The sunshine warmed my face and was a welcome feeling. Birds dove through the air from tree to tree like stealth fighters. You could smell the vibrancy of life in the air. The backpack I carried felt light as the straps caressed my shoulders. The three books and laptop were nothing compared to the full battle rattle and pack I'd become accustomed to wearing. After the mission, I was awarded the Silver Star for rescuing Staff Sergeant Stewart and orchestrating the evacuation of the mission that had almost gone to hell in a busted ass wicker basket. I had ended up serving ten years in the Army, most of those years in Special Operations. My training had made me one of the best at what I did, as noted by my DD-214, discharge paperwork and the accolades of my peers.

The years spent honing the skills needed to survive, evade, resist and escape any and every threat had left me with a resume that was not exactly useful in the world outside of being hired as an elite badass. Sure, I could have been a police officer, mercenary or even bodyguard for some spoiled ass, saggy pants-, shitty haircut-wearing pop singer, but the problem with that was that the rules of engagement in the civilian sector were far different from the Army. There were too many restrictions on what you could and couldn't do when you were a lethal babysitter. And, although I have the utmost respect for them, being a police officer was never my style: there are too many rules and not enough forgiveness for my style of information acquisition.

I had decided to use my G.I. Bill and go back to school. I enrolled at Utah State University after moving back to Logan, Utah the fall after being honorably discharged. I had always been a fan of the mountains, and Logan seemed to have it all. The Rocky Mountains were my style and provided the free weekend therapy I very much needed. I had a slack ass Bachelor's degree from Utah State that I had earned before the military and had returned to put my knowledge to some good use and get an actual, functional degree that I could use in the real world. Being thirty-six years old had its advantages, though: The thrill of frat parties and underage sneaky drinking that had plagued me in my youth were no longer an issue; not only could I drink legally now, I actually preferred to sit in a chair around a bonfire and sip a whiskey or the occasional Michelob Ultra—a stark contrast to the beer pong and keggers of before. I was also in better shape than most other students, minus some of the athletes, and carried myself in a way that garnered attention from the female species without even trying. However, I couldn't handle the drama that came with the younger crowds and so I opted to keep my distance from the campus social life.

My classes were all fairly easy. The homework was light and not much of a challenge. I had decided that I wanted to grow up and be an environmental engineer. It was a perfect match for me. I had spent much of my youth in the mountains and felt at home when lost in the woods. One of the classes I had enrolled in was an Environmental Ethics class. I never imagined that the class would change my life forever—both now and in the life after this—but, somehow, I think my professor did. At the time, I figured I was merely crossing off another class from my To Do list.

The first day of classes was filled with a buzz that signaled the end of a long summer and the commencement of the social escapade that is college life. I joined my peers in filing into the classroom and climbed the short stairs to the middle of the stadium seating. The classroom could hold just over 150 students, but class had maybe thirty students at most. I always sat in the back of most public places. I had an incessant need to see everyone and everything that was happening around me. This had become a typical thing in today's society as more and more people were coming back from deployments overseas. It's a need to control all that you can by sitting with your back against the wall at a restaurant. It's the need to keep everything around you in front of you so that you can control what happens next and thereby eliminate the possibility of a surprise coming from behind you.

As students began to fill more of the seats in the classroom, there was an electricity that filled the air. Being an upper-level class, most of the students had been in classes with each other at one time or another and made casual conversation, catching up on their summer adventures. The students had all but finished trickling into the class when a woman in her early-thirties walked in. She carried a worn leather backpack and looked every bit of a student as the others, but she took her place at the front of the room and set her pack on the floor behind the desk that sat upfront. Her brown hair was pulled back in a hasty bun, showing her cinnamon skin. Her sunglasses sat on her face as she scanned the room with a gentle smile. Her thin lips ever so slightly moved as she appeared to count the bodies in the room. She slid her glasses from her face, revealing soft, blue eyes. She stood tall, giving herself an aura of invincibility while at once appearing very feminine. She didn't dress much like any professor I had seen before; her shirt was a long-sleeve button down that was tied at the front with the sleeves rolled once or twice, showing her wrists and lower arms. A small sliver of her tanned stomach peeked through the shirt and her Levi cutoffs. Her legs, tanned like the rest of her, stretched from the frayed ends of the cutoff shorts to a pair of Chaco sandals that were strapped to her feet. The small dragon fly tattoo on her left ankle was barely visible through her sun-kissed skin. She was not a prissy girl, and her well-defined muscle tone gave concluding evidence of such.

"Good afternoon everyone," she opened. "I am Dr. Amber Lockhart, but please call me Amber. I'm not much for formalities, and just because I have a piece of paper that proves I majored in low-income student loans doesn't mean I'm going to ask you to call me *Doctor*."

Her smile and nonchalant attitude immediately put the room at ease. Some professors would stand at the front of the classroom and brag their credentials to the student body as if there were royalty claiming their lineage. Dr. Lockhart— *Amber*—was clearly very different. She stood tall and was sure of herself, but her eyes bore a fire that radiated peace and softness. She scanned the classroom, stopping for a brief second to make eye contact with each student. She wore her smile the entire time she looked over the group, blanketing us with a palpable calm. The first-day anxiety and jitters were pretty minimal at this stage in our education, but her approach was nonetheless welcomed.

The typical first day of class consists of going over the syllabus and finding alignment between the expectations of students and professor alike. Amber bypassed all of that and went straight to the topic of the day, which was what we'd all done over the summer vacation. As elementary as it sounded, it was a great ice breaker. After a few chuckles, one or two students offered answers of world travel and epic tales of conquest at the beach that were fought during the summer months. To this point, Amber had relied on students to volunteer their answers. A brief moment of silence signaled what seemed to be the end of the discussion.

"What about you? What did *you* do during your summer vacation?"

I was looking down at the scribbles of time-passing in my notebook and only looked up when the silence of the class became deafening. The stares of thirty students bore into my skull. Dr. Lockhart's eyes locked onto mine as I looked up. I wasn't much for volunteering information. My situational awareness was still intact as I sat back and gathered intel on my surroundings. I quickly studied the students, their body language and mannerisms. *Time to adapt, overcome, and improvise, Orion*, I thought.

"Um, yeah... My name is Orion, and this summer I, uh..." My thoughts raced through the various foreign countries, the small villages, the numerous doors kicked in. I flashed to the many flights in and out of each satellite hell along the way.

I remembered the last firefight and carrying Marcus out of the chaos. I saw the wings, lit and protective, and thought of the events that had saved our lives that day. "I, uh, spent some time with my toes in the sand." I couldn't exactly tell the story of how my kill ratio rivaled that of the first wave of the bubonic plague. I wasn't exactly lying, either: my toes *had* been in the sand at some point along the way, notably in one of the missions to Iraq early on in the year. "I did a little hiking and hunting in the mountains," I finished—again, not a lie.

Amber didn't take her eyes off mine once. "Hmm, sounds like you tried to let your free spirit take over this summer." Her eyes continued to hold mine like she was trying to read the most inner parts of me. I could tell she didn't buy my story, but she played it off in front of the other students. As she broke her gaze and looked down at a pile of papers she had on the desk in front of her, her lips began to grow a small yet sly smile. She entertained a few other stories from students—drunken debauchery, small town soirees and the like—before moving on to explaining a bit about the class.

Throughout her class, I noticed that Amber was a very sturdy woman. She was formal in her speech and her grammar was perfect. She looked whomever she was talking to directly in the eyes and gave them her full attention. She never showed any sign of female insecurity or weakness that could have garnered attention from the males in the classroom.

I wondered if her father had been military or perhaps maybe even she had served in some capacity. It was rare to see someone so proper yet silently formidable. But then I reasoned she might just be one of those diamonds in the rough.

When she came to close her class, she gave us a couple chapters to read over in our predetermined textbook before excusing us. The bustle of students began to shuffle out of the classroom as they gathered their gear. As I slung my pack on my back and walked down the classroom stairs and towards the door, I heard the good doctor's voice call out, "Orion, can I talk to you for a second?" I turned to answer and saw her making her way to me at the door. "I would love to hear more about your summer adventures, if you have some time. Maybe we could grab lunch?" I couldn't get over the depth of blue in her eyes. They were the deepest, softest blue with a ring of dark grey on their outer edge. I was mesmerized, and I swear as I looked into them I could see the color swirl ever so slightly.

"There's not much to tell, Doctor Lo—*Amber*," I correct myself. "Just a lot of time spent outdoors, taking in the scenery." There's no way she had the clearance needed for me to tell her about the things that we were tasked with, not to mention I wasn't the type to kiss and tell of my military exploits.

She gave me a quick hand on the shoulder tap like she was one of the guys. "A summer in the mountains and time on the beach and not much to tell?" She smiled a devious smile before leaning in close and whispering, "Did you see Bigfoot? Did he touch you down there?" She quietly whispered as she dropped her gaze before bringing it back to my eyes. "It's okay, you're in a safe place now, Orion. I won't say a word."

I burst into laughter. Amber had put me at ease from the moment she'd asked about my summer during class. She just had something about her that I couldn't explain—and had also showed me she had a twisted sense of humor.

She stepped back and gave a small laugh before continuing. "I'm kidding. Listen, I'll settle for coffee if you'd rather, but I'd like to hear about it. Interested?"

How could I say no? "Lunch? Okay, I'm game. Your class is my last of the day. Where and when?" There was no way I could pass on this. Beautiful, intriguing woman? Check. Irreverent sense of humor? Check. Enough balls to ask *me* out? Check. Alright, coach, take me out of the game. I'm done.

"I've got to make some phonecalls and take care of a few things back in my office. Let's meet in an hour at Morty's, that little sandwich joint on the edge of campus. Deal?" Her confidence game was so strong that she knew I would say yes and began walking down the hall. "Deal," I said under my breath. She was a drug and I was instantly addicted.

I blew out of the door to the outside world with an unrivaled sense of swagger. The outside world was an explosion of color and life. I was the little girl in the Blind Melon "No Rain" video. The little girl awkwardly dressed in a bee costume who was all alone and understood by nobody; the little girl who wandered the town seemingly aimlessly, talking to people but none of them truly able to 'get' her. I felt the same way about life outside of the military and going back to school. But then, fast-forward to later on in the video, and the little girl in the bee costume sees other people dressed like bees. She is ecstatic that she's no longer alone.

Amber was somebody else in a bee costume.

I walked out into the courtyard, making my way to Morty's where I was going to meet Amber in just under an hour's time. I was only a couple blocks away, and if I hurried I could make it there and get some studying done before she showed up.

I reached Morty's and found that, thankfully, it wasn't too busy. I chose a table on the balcony overlooking part of the campus. I sat my bag down and pulled out one of my books for class while I enjoyed the sun across my face. I would stop and look around at the students every few moments and find it difficult to focus; I'm not sure if it was the constant bustle of life going on around me or if it was the excitement of meeting Amber. People-watching had become more than a hobby for me. It was all part of a lifestyle that I couldn't shake; needing to know everyone and everything going on around me, not to mention that watching other people was more entertaining and humorous than almost anything on TV these days.

"Excuse me, sir," a voice said, breaking into my thoughts, "I'm going to have to ask you to move. This table is reserved for a party of two." I looked up to find that the pseudo hostess was Amber. Her soft laugh immediately followed, and she took a seat at the table with me.

"Reservations, eh?" I tried to stay serious, but she had a way of putting me at ease so very easily.

"Did you order yet?" Amber asked as she gathered her hair off her shoulders and collected it at the back.

"No, I was waiting for you. Shall we?" I got up from my chair and motioned my arm forward in a gentleman-like offering. After ordering and getting our food, we made our way back up to the balcony and sat at our table.

"So, what's your story, Orion? Where are you from?" Amber wasn't your typical shy girl when it came to eating. She had ordered a chicken sandwich and was making it her bitch. She was very athletically toned, and so I felt it safe to assume that she worked her ass off to compensate.

She asked her questions and immediately engulfed a bite of her monster sandwich. We made small talk and I told her a little about my younger years. I became somewhat evasive when I got to my years in the service and neglected to mention the fact that I had served. I was proud of my service, but I wasn't one of those 'throw it in your face, give me my military discount' types.

"So, Orion, what's your major? What do you want to be when you grow up?" Taking another bite of her food, she turned her eyes to me, patiently waiting for me to answer.

I explained my reasoning for pursuing environmental engineering. I gave her the cliff notes version of loving the mountains and having a desire to help preserve that. A small window of silence permeated as we enjoyed a few bites of food.

"Orion, how many tours did you do?" She took another bite and acted nonchalant about her surprise question. That sly smirk was once again starting to creep across her lips, but stayed mostly at bay.

"What makes you think I was military?" I asked, knowing full well the possible obvious reasons for her to assume as much. I waited to hear her take on the assumption.

"Come on, Orion. You're built like a Mack truck. Your arms look like Serena William's thighs. You have tats down to your elbows—on *both* sides. You're thirty-six and pursuing your second Bachelor's. You're not cocky, but carry yourself with security and demand respect just by walking into a room. It's not hard to decipher."

She'd clearly been paying attention. She was a very observant woman, but then again, anyone paying attention could probably put the pieces together.

"How do you know so much about the military?" I'd figured it was due to the prevalence of PTSD and the news stories in recent years. Immediately after I asked the question, however, her sly smile softened and she turned to look off into the distance.

"My brother was a Marine with the First Recon Battalion. They were in the Helmand province, Afghanistan on September 28, 2011 when the group he was with was attacked. He was killed. It was just him and me. He was my best friend. I know that sounds weird to say about your big brother, but that's how it was. We did everything together." She turned back to face me and smiled. "When he needed someone to throw a baseball to him so he could practice hitting, I learned to pitch. When he needed help throwing the football to practice catching, I learned passing routes. When I needed help stretching and conditioning for dance, he was there as my personal trainer. Our family grew up with very little money and a whole lotta love." She smiled. "We were close." Her eyes began to well slightly, but no tears fell. She flashed a full smile, and I could tell that, not only did she miss her brother, but she was still so proud of him.

"I'm sorry you lost your brother. He sounds like he was an amazing guy and one hell of a Marine."

It was one of those awkward moments that almost commanded that I reach out and hug her—or at least take her hand in a comforting gesture—but I didn't know Amber that well. Besides, she seemed different from the other family members of fallen service members I'd talked to; she didn't appear at all vulnerable in her moment of reflection.

"He wouldn't want any pity, and neither would I," she said, confirming my thoughts as she turned her eyes back up to meet mine and continued her smile.

"I offer no pity, just gratitude."

I expected an awkward silence to follow such a somber topic, but Amber acted as if nothing was wrong and moved on.

"You remind me a lot of my brother, Orion," she said. I think you would have gotten along with him—both born for the military, but humble." Her lips kissed the straw of her iced tea and her eyes lightened.

"It sounds like you've done a little research on me, Dr. Lockhart. Stalk much?" We both laughed a little and she surprisingly didn't deny it.

"Hey, I wanted to know who and what I was dealing with as far as students go. I admit that I find you mildly attractive, and—"

"Mildly?" I interjected.

"Okay, you're pretty damn hot." She laughed, an almost wicked glint in her eye. "I don't mind telling you that, before I met you here, I was in my office checking your student account and cyber stalking you to see if you had Facebook, Twitter, any of those platforms. You don't have a Facebook page, but the VA liaison—my good friend Russ Beckman—was more than helpful in giving me enough for now."

"Dr. Lockhart, I'm ashamed of you." I winked at her and sarcastically chastised her, knowing that, in all likelihood, using school equipment and personnel to find out the personal details of any student would be against policy. "Your actions today warrant punishment up to and including a date with me tonight." I wasn't upset at all and she knew it.

She gave an over-the-top eye roll. "Oh, please, suck it up, Princess. Besides, you can't sit here and tell me you haven't done your fair share of research for intel on your professors." She seemed to know me better than most despite only having met me two hours before.

We wrapped up our lunch date and made plans for me to pick her up at 7 PM. We exchanged numbers and she texted me her address. We bid goodbye and I gave her a friendly side hug. Her sun-tipped brown hair smelled like coconut and her hands were soft yet firm against my back. She turned to walk away and made it about ten steps before she turned her head and gave an ever so slight look back. I hadn't moved from the spot where I'd held the door open for her.

I was 1990 Charlie Sheen and she was cocaine. And I knew I was hooked.

The drive home was a blur of thoughts and deeply hidden emotions that I hadn't allowed to surface for years. I had dated on and off, but it wasn't something I'd ever actively pursued. Having worked in Texas on the oil rigs before joining the military, the typical women I'd come across had seemed to be after just one thing: oil field money. And then, after I joined the Army, I was busy with training for the first few years. I had never been up for the typical 'go out on the weekends and tap anything with a heartbeat' type. Sure, I went out, but I was living out a childhood fantasy, and I put my whole heart into that. After joining Special Operations, my social life had been limited to hanging out with the guys when we were stateside, as if we were a secluded, loyal family. These feelings were now seeing the light of day after a long, deep hibernation, and although I wanted to keep them guarded, I just couldn't help but let them thrive.

I opened the door to my house and threw my keys on the kitchen counter. I'd bought the three-bedroom, one-and-a-half bath home a week before classes had started, and so there were still boxes here and there, waiting to be unpacked. The house was set on about a third acre—enough room for a dog to run or to host a barbecue or even grow a garden perfect—in an area of town known as 'The Island'. While the rest of Logan was in the foothills of the immense and surrounding mountains, The Island was an approximate twenty-five square mile area that was like a bowl; sloping down to form what was almost like its own little village in the middle of Logan. I'd got a great deal on the house and picked it up for $30,000 under market. The owners were an older couple who had actually built the house way back in 1926. It was well taken care of and had been updated to comprise modern electrical, plumbing and insulation. It was perfect for the bachelor life, and yet it still had room to grow in the future.

I turned the shower on and let the water warm while I stripped down to my boxers. Setting my phone on the counter by the sink, I opened up my Spotify app and turned on a mellow mix of Country. I walked into the kitchen—appreciating living the single life and being able to wander the house in nothing but underwear—and grabbed a beer from the fridge for in the shower. Of course, I'd heard of "shower beer" before and laughed it off until I'd tried it. Somehow, someway, it gives a better tasting beer.

Slipping my boxers off and stepping into the shower with my can of Michelob Ultra, my mind continued to spin as I contemplated life and the classes I was taking, but no matter what thoughts ran through my mind, Amber's face would always flash to the forefront.

Turning the water off, I grabbed a towel to pat myself dry when my phone rang. I looked to see the caller ID and didn't recognize the number. Damn telemarketers had started calling people's cell phones now. If I could thank the person who started invading America's privacy by telemarketing to the cell phones of its citizen, I'd do it with a brick. To the face.

I figured I would keep the date that evening pretty casual; jeans, and a button down dress shirt but untucked with the sleeves rolled up. Cowboy boots, of course. I'd planned to take her to a little spot in town called The White Owl. It was a bar and was by no means fancy; rather, it was very low key and had six pool tables and a jukebox, but they served the best damn hamburgers in the state. They served them with chips and a pickle that had been soaked in jalapeno juice. The meal was probably two-thousand calories by itself, but it was so worth it.

Picking up my phone, I turned off the music and slid it into my back pocket. I had to run and pick up my mail that was being held at the post office across town. I'd my mail forwarded, but it hadn't quite kicked in yet, and the post office was going to keep anything for me there until the beginning of the next week. I hopped in my 2017 Toyota Tundra that I called Betty, as in Black Betty. The truck was black, and I'd put on black rims, black steprails, and black interior accents. It was black on black on black. LL Cool J would be proud. It was lifted an extra four inches and the tires were thirty-five inches extra wide. It had a mean, wide stance for a Tundra. The only thing was she had a drinking problem: the mileage wasn't bad for a truck and sat around 15 mpg, but she sure sucked it up driving around town.

I drove to the post office and picked up my mail. There were mostly ads, a letter from the VA, and a statement from the Utilities department. Nothing to get too excited about. As I walked out of the post office, I saw an elderly lady sitting at the bus stop about thirty yards away. She was holding a large bouquet of flowers as she got in line to get on the bus. I'd seen her around town and in front of the supermarkets selling flowers, just like the ones she was holding. She wore clothes that seemed to be at least two sizes too big, and they were frayed at the edges. I guessed she'd got a hold of these flowers somehow and sold them to try and make a living. I rushed over to her and tapped her on the shoulder.

"Excuse me, ma'am, how much for a flower?" The flowers were tulips but all varied in color, from white, yellow and red to orange and even purple. However, stuck in the middle of the bunch was a single daisy; it was a vibrant white against the palette of tulips.

"Three dollars each or twenty-five for a dozen."

I cringed inside. That was one hell of a markup. Even I could make a living from that kind of inflation. I pulled a twenty from my wallet and gave it to her as I pulled the one single daisy from her bunch. Having an internal dialogue with myself, I figured that at least she was trying to do what she had to do to provide for her family—if, in fact, she had a family. After taking the daisy, I gave her a wink and turned back to my truck. I figured one flower wouldn't be too much of an overkill for Amber, but would still be a simple, sweet gesture. Setting it on the seat beside me, I turned out of the parking lot and headed towards her address.

When I pulled up to the townhouse, I grabbed the daisy and hopped out. Her place was in a newer part of town, and the townhouses looked like they'd only recently been finished. There was no lawn as yet, and I could see construction debris to the side of the building.

I knocked and heard a muffled "Come in" from inside.

Cautiously opening the door and entering, I found boxes stacked inside the living room and the kitchen. Just beyond the front living room looked like Ikea had exploded. There was shit everywhere.

"Hey! Sorry about the mess. I just moved in and I haven't had any time to put anything away." She came down the stairs and slowly put her hands around my neck in a quick hug-like fashion. She had on a pair of shorts, but not the cut-off ones from earlier; these looked like some Old Navy summer shorts, and they had an intended hem on the bottom. Her shirt was a simple white summer blouse that complimented her very well. She smiled at me and gave me a scrunched up nose wink before looking at the flower I held. "Orion Thorrsen, did you buy this lil ol' girl a flower?" Her voice adopted a southern drawl as she took on a "Gone with the Wind" persona.

"Yes, ma'am. I did just that." I handed it over, and she took it to the kitchen. Searching through boxes she said something about finding a 'damn vase' in one of the 'damn boxes'. As she continued to look, she explained that she had just moved from another apartment she'd lived in. These were newer and in a quieter neighborhood. The price was right and she claimed that she couldn't pass it up. She finally found a vase that she claimed would work and filled it with water. After setting the flower in the vase and placing it in the center of the table that sat in her dining area, she hurried back to the living room, grabbed her purse from a stack of boxes, and took my arm as she continued out the door. I opened the truck door for her and watched her step up and slide inside.

The bar wasn't too busy, and the crowd was already showing the excitement of Friday and the start of school. After ordering two beers at the bar, I took Amber up the stairs that led to the balcony on top of the building. It was a redwood deck patio with twelve round tables, each covered with an umbrella. They had a small beer tap bar on one side that was flanked by a grill, which was filled with flame-broiled burgers. We found a table and settled in.

We talked a little more about each other's pasts. She explained how she had come to teach and the path to her doctorates. I talked about growing up in California and bouncing back and forth between there and Utah. The sun was starting to set and the sky began to glow with an orange warmth. There was never an awkward silence between us and the conversations seemed to flow naturally.

Already I admired her cool, calm, self-confidence. She seemed to know exactly what she wanted out of life and never seemed to waiver on anything, whether it was ordering food or pursuing her dream of teaching and environmental research. The night gently eased on, and we flowed from one subject to another between eating our burgers and ordering drinks. It was dark outside and the deck was lit by white fairy lights that had been strung above, zig-zagging across from one end to the other. The warm summer night was a relief and the ambience was well set.

Amber looked down at her watch, noting that it was now ten-thirty.

"Do you have a curfew, Dr. Lockhart?" I asked sarcastically.

She laughed and never said a word before flipping me off and continuing to laugh.

The music from the bar below crept up the stairs to the deck and mixed with the crowd that had found their way outside. There wasn't an empty table to be found, and the remaining chairs around our table had been borrowed by other tables and their groups to accommodate extra guests.

"Hey, do you want to get out of here? We can head back to my place and watch a movie if that's cool?" I wasn't the biggest fan of crowds and much preferred the solitude of a couch and good company over eleventy-four other people I didn't know crammed onto a deck forty-feet above the street.

"Are you asking me to *Netflix and chill*, Orion? What kind of girl do you take me for?" Her beautiful smile flashed, and before I could defend myself she told me she was just giving me shit. "Yeah, let's get out of here," she yelled over the crowd.

We stood up and, as I turned towards the stairs, I took her hand. Her warm, smooth skin felt natural against my own. Our fingers interlocked, and I led us through the crowd down the stairs.

The drive was short as I only lived two miles from the bar. I parked and we both hopped out, making our way to the front of the truck. As Amber looked up to me, she reached her hand to mine and took it in hers. Not a word was said as we walked from the driveway and up the porch stairs.

Sliding the key into the lock I turned to her. "I just moved in here a little bit ago and am still unpacking, too. It's not quite the shit show you have going on over at your place, but please pardon the mess." Chuckling as I opened the door, she slapped my arm and moved me inside.

I flipped on the lights and gave her a quick tour of the place. As we made our way back to the living room after the grand tour, we stopped and found ourselves looking into each other's eyes, not saying a word. It was unspoken but known by both of us that this was the part where we would kiss.

I took her face in my hands and leaned down, tilting my head to the side. My eyes darting from her eyes to her mouth, I closed them in anticipation of tasting her lips. She gently embraced me, her lips parting ever so slightly as we both immersed ourselves into the magic of the moment. Her hands raised and she rested them on my arms. All rational thoughts had stopped. Our kiss began to build momentum as our tongues met and tasted one another, the kiss growing ever deeper and more passionate.

The TV didn't get turned on that night. Not one movie was watched. We collapsed on the couch and wrapped ourselves in the moment and each other. The weightlessness of the moment lasted for hours. We were tuned into each other's soul and knew just where to touch, where to kiss. Instincts seemed to tell us when to push and when to pull as our bodies moved, never once stopping to guess at what to do next. The calculated and precise movements were orchestrated by a seemingly predetermined knowledge of this lustful dance.

I knew that this was the beginning. Throughout the night and for the many nights to come, we acted as if we'd been dating for years. Our personalities meshed so perfectly that there was never a questionable period as to what we were. We were definitely dating and, after a few weeks, we both just assumed the roles that we were born to fill of boyfriend and girlfriend.

CHAPTER 4

It had taken me a couple weeks, but I had finally unpacked the last of the boxes and made the house a half-ass home. I had started to work on the yard and was in the middle of clearing an area for a firepit. School was now in the routine stage, and classes, research papers, exams and studying were all part of the day. Amber taught her last class at 3 PM and finished up in her office for an hour before coming over to my house for the late-night part of the routine. She had moved into her townhouse just before the term started, but over the last four weeks that we had been unofficially official, she had only spent a total of two weeks there.

We had begun a few rituals, one of them being Taco Tuesdays. We both loved to cook and, more times than not, it became foreplay for us. With both of us loving Mexican food, Taco Tuesdays were inevitable. I had most of the ingredients already, and texted her asking if she could stop by the store for sour cream on her way over. I had started cooking the hamburger and was chopping the lettuce when I heard a light knock at the door and the creak of it opening.

Amber had made herself welcome after we met and she knew—I'm sure because of her brother and the military life—that it was a real good idea to announce your arrival when walking in.

"Hey, sexy, need some cream?" Her sing-song voice floated through the air as she walked in to the kitchen and set the bag on the counter. I put the knife down and wiped my hands on the towel that was draped over my shoulder. I typically cooked without a shirt on because, well... guys do that thing from time to time.

I wrapped my arms around her waist and picked her up as our lips came together in passion. Her lips tasted like eucalyptus from her lip balm, and the flavor tasted better than usual as a low toned moan growled in her throat.

"You can keep your cream. I'd rather have the whole cow." I didn't have time to give her the playful wink before she smacked the back of my head, calling me an asshole. Her face twisted into an angry knot of emotion, but quickly eased into a playful smile. I had told her from the very first night that I admired her body. The dedication it took to take such great care of herself and keep in the condition she was in was no small task.

We kissed again as I set her down, and we went about finishing preparing the taco bar. Once everything was placed at the table, she picked up a bottle of wine to go along with dinner and pulled the cork on it. I couldn't help but laugh as she poured the wine into two plastic cups she pulled out of the cupboard. Most people wouldn't pair a Moscato with their Taco Tuesday, let alone use plastic cups.

"I've got a question for you, babe," I said as I finished the last bite of my soft taco. "I was wondering if you, uh, wanted to be my roommate..."

I'd thought about it since the first night. Everything with Amber felt so natural. I told myself that, if I had denied that, I'd be going against fate and the universe.

She slowly lowered her taco to her plate. "Is this just your way of trying to get the cream for free instead of paying for it?" Her lips curled, and she wore the sarcasm like a mask. I couldn't help but lean back in my chair and laugh out loud. She had just as quick wit as I did.

"What? I would never!" Her exaggerated nod kept me laughing for a minute longer. "Amber, listen... We've been together for roughly four weeks. You're over here more than you are your own place. Besides, if I'm being completely honest, I know that this is completely right. This is what the universe has in store for us. From the first night, I've never once questioned it. It's you. The universe has spoken and it's you." The exaggeration was gone and the sarcasm put aside.

Her eyes softened, and I could see her bottom lip give a slight shake as her eyes began to wet. "Ry, I just moved in to my townhouse and signed a one-year contract. What would we do about that?" She'd used 'we' before when talking about her and I, but this time it felt real. True.

"We can find someone to take over your contract. If not, I'm sure there's a buyout penalty. We can find somebody to take over for you or just pay the owner and let them deal with filling it. It's ridiculous to keep paying the rent when you could move in here. My house is paid for anyway. It'd save us money." I had rationalized the topic for three days now. I didn't mind paying the penalty fee, if there was one, if it meant it streamlined our lives.

Silence lingered for what seemed like never-ending minutes as her wetted eyes stared into my soul. I reached for her and felt the small shock of warmth as I took her hand. Through the tear that was creeping to the corner of her eye, I saw it. That look. The hunger was growling deep within the both of us, and it was about to break free. In a furious haste, my grip tightened on her hand as we both stood up. Pulling her around the edge of the table and into my arms, I lifted her up and set her on the table with my right hand as I cleared the table with a quick swipe of my left hand.

"Hungry for more than tacos, are you?" Slicing her words edgewise in between the kisses, I knew that her rhetorical question needed no answering. In a calculated movement, she raised her arms and at the same time I lifted her shirt off of her, tossing it to the floor amongst what was left of Taco Tuesday. Cooking was foreplay *and* dessert? Well, dessert was always so sweet with Amber.

We had moved to the bedroom and, as I lay on my back catching my breath, Amber moved to my side and lay her head on my outstretched arm. "Were you serious about me moving in?" Amber softly asked. I knew that *she* knew I was serious. I think I said it for my own reassurance as well. I had never had a girlfriend whose relationship had moved to this level. It was a big step for the both of us. "I'm dead serious. Amber, I'm so in love with you. I've never been this happy in my life and I don't think it's right of us to fight the powers that be when they did all that work to line up the planets in our favor."

She called her landlord the next morning and let him know the situation. He was more than accommodating and said he had a waiting list for the townhouse so filling it wouldn't be a problem. Amber began moving in the very next day. Most of her things were still in boxes because, according to her, it didn't make sense to move them from one storage place to another. Yup, she was my yang.

Amber and I had begun to live the cohabitating lifestyle to the fullest. She worked while I went to school during the week. This was made easy by the G. I. Bill, which not only paid for my tuition, but gave me a stipend each month as well. That, in addition to the fact I owned my home and had no debt, allowed me to study and focus on school only. I'd saved a large chunk of money while in the Army; there was no real need for me to spend money because they paid for my housing, food, uniforms, and all utilities.

On the weekends, we hopped in the truck and took off somewhere. Sometimes it was deep in the mountains, sometimes it was southwest to the desert for some four-wheeling. During one of the semester breaks, we drove to Vegas and then on to California where we went to Disneyland. Amber had never been, and acted like a little kid the whole time. I had never seen her so giddy. I made sure she rode all of the classic rides, like Pirates of the Caribbean, The Haunted Mansion, It's a Small World, and the Matterhorn. It had been more than ten years since I'd been and I was amazed at the work that had been done at California Adventures. We walked Downtown Disney and bounced from shop to shop for a couple hours on our last day at the park before deciding to take off and go to the beach. I had always felt at home at the beach. The power of the water brought peace to my soul.

One Friday evening, Amber and I had decided to Netflix and chill at home and not go anywhere. While surfing the movies we would more than likely not make it completely through, I asked Amber if she saw herself in this moment, right now.

"What do you mean? Like, with you?" She half turned her head toward me, but kept her eyes on the scrolling movies to choose from.

I slid my hand to the small of her back and gently rubbed as she leaned forward, studying the choices available.

"I mean, did you ever picture your life like this right now? You, a professor teaching Environmental Ethics among other subjects, living the life of sin with a jobless vet?"

Her hands dropped as she laughed and fully turned to face me. "If this is sin, then send me to Hell, Captain." Her eyes softened in the way they always did, and she sat silence for another few moments before continuing. "I always wanted to teach, to help others understand and love the world around them. So, that? Yeah, I totally saw that part. It was you that I never saw coming. I thought I had my life figured out when I was twenty-two. I was accepted as an intern-slash teacher's assistant, and I was engaged to my high school boyfriend whom I'd dated off and on since our sophomore year."

Shock washed over my face as I stammered, "Whoa... What? You were engaged?"

Amber turned her body to face me straight-on and, with her hands raised slightly and resting on my chest, said, "Orion, I didn't tell you because it wasn't the best time of my life. In fact, there was one night where I didn't think I would see the next morning."

It wasn't the fact she was engaged that had surprised me; I couldn't be upset that she was engaged or, hell, even married before she met me. We were both living different lives then. The only thing that mattered as far as that went was that she was with me now. The part that got me was that she had never told me about it.

"Amber, it's fine. That was your past and we didn't even know each other. I just don't understand why you didn't tell me." The thought that maybe she didn't trust me with such a significant piece of information hurt—there was definitely a little pain there.

"His name was Paul Griffith. We met in high school and dated for the better part of three years up until graduation. After graduation he went to the University of Utah on a football scholarship. I was accepted there too, and we'd planned to continue dating. We each lived in the dorms, but not the same one. Things were going along just fine as I was going to school and the season had started for him. It was the fourth game of the year and they were playing Air Force at home. He played second string receiver and had been put in the game after the guy that was in front of him had dropped two passes. The Utes had the ball and he ran twenty yards out when the ball was thrown to him. Paul jumped up to catch it and when he came down with it, he turned to run it up the field. He got about three steps when a player for the Falcons blindsided him and knocked him out cold. He lay there on the field and didn't move. The trainers, coaches and medical staff ran out to check on him. Once he came to, they loaded him on a stretcher and took him to the hospital because he couldn't feel his legs".

"Jesus..." Of course, I'd seen my share of injuries—both my own and those of others—on the field, as well as in the military. "He'd cracked a vertebra in his neck, which ended up compressing a nerve going to his legs. Eventually he regained feeling in his legs and, after little more than a year of physical therapy, he was given the all clear. The only condition was that he would never be able to play football—or any contact sport, for that matter—again.

"During that year of therapy, we'd grown together as a couple and he proposed to me after school had let out for the summer that next year. We started planning the wedding for the holiday season later that same year and wanted to get married just after Thanksgiving but before Christmas. What I didn't know was that Paul had become addicted to pain pills during that time. In the beginning he'd take them as he was told to, but he started to crave that feeling, I guess, and ended up taking double, then triple the amount he should have after a few months."

I slowly shook my head; I knew that opioids addiction was a growing epidemic, and it wasn't uncommon to hear about someone becoming hooked.

"So, you left him when he became addicted?"

"Not exactly. I started to notice things, like empty pill bottles in his car when he shouldn't have been out of them. He'd miss physical therapy appointments and classes, which wasn't like him at all. No, I didn't leave him because he got addicted. I left him because his problem spiraled out of control and he couldn't function without the pills. He started drinking heavily and mixing the two.

"I left him because, one night, I went over to his dorm room and tried to ask him—beg him, actually—to get help." Amber looked down, and I could tell she was trying to hide the tears that were starting to well. Her now shaking voice continued, "That night, he was worse than I'd ever seen him. He started yelling and throwing things, screaming at me to 'stay the fuck out' of his business and that he didn't have a problem. I stood up and told him that if he wanted to marry me he'd need to get help; I said I refused to live with an alcoholic drug addict. That's when he hit me. I could see his face redden as he stopped yelling and looked at me with a face that I didn't recognize. I hadn't seen that side of him before. I saw him pull his fist back and the next thing I remember was waking up in my own bed. He'd taken me back to my dorm room but not before beating me so bad that both of my eyes had swollen shut. He shattered my right eye socket and my ear drum had ruptured."

I could feel my body tense up. My heart went from sorrow and sympathy to anger and rage. Her tears had not only begun to fall, but they had continued to stream down her face. I could tell it wasn't from fear or remembrance of being beaten; the tears fell from a much deeper place of hurt.

"There was bruising both internally and outside. He had continued to pummel me until he got his fill and then apparently picked me up, drove me over to my dorm, carried me in and dumped me on the bed." She wasn't sobbing any more. Her voice was steady. This woman had somehow gained strength after this tragic event and no longer seemed to be victimized by it.

"Baby, what happened after that?" I didn't want to overstep my bounds, and only wanted to hear the parts she was comfortable telling me. It was all I could do to bow up and ask her if she called the cops, called her brother, her dad—somebody.

She looked down, took a slow, deep breath, and continued. "I woke up looking like hell. I tried to wash my face to get the blood off so that maybe I could open my eyes enough to drive. I tried, but I was too swollen. I stumbled back to the bed and reached for my phone that was on the nightstand. I called my house and my dad answered. He came to get me and took me to the hospital. After getting me checked in they asked a barrage of questions. Was I raped? Did I know the attacker? Was there a weapon used? They started treating me while I answered questions. I got an IV, they took x rays, the whole deal. What I didn't know was that, during that time of being treated, my dad went to 'talk' to Paul". When she said *talk*, she made little quotation marks in the air.

I knew from our conversations that Amber's family had a rich military history and her father had served as a Marine in Vietnam. I could see where this was going.

"I guess my dad had grabbed his service weapon from the house and brought it with him when he picked me up. He left the hospital and drove to Paul's dorm, but Paul had already left. He'd packed some clothes and taken off. I guess he figured he was better off disappearing on his own terms than on somebody else's. For years nobody knows where he went that night. He resurfaced in town about three years ago—or so I heard. I'm sure if my dad and brother were alive they would have found him and taken care of things then."

She fell silent, tears slowing their stream down her cheeks. I reached to wipe them off and gently took her head in my hand and guided her to me. I set her against my chest and laid back on the couch.

I wanted to protect this woman from everything, even her past. I couldn't imagine her beautiful face brutally beaten to that point, nor did I want to. She pulled her feet on to the couch and tucked them behind her as she curled up in my lap.

We talked for hours after that. She told me it was that night that changed her life for the better. I couldn't understand until she explained that after three weeks she had healed enough that she felt comfortable enough to go out in public. She had been granted a leave of absence from school and moved back to Logan with her family. She started taking Tae Kwon Do classes and learned how to defend herself. She said she damn sure she wasn't going to let that happen to her again—or anybody else if she could help it. After fourteen years, she had grown up a completely different woman. She was strong, determined, fierce; that explained the way she carried herself. She walked with an assuredness. She was strong, both physically and mentally. She had beaten the stigma and the mold of domestic violence victims. She had come out on top when such a thing was and still is rare.

Our conversation had begun to die out and we eventually fell asleep, her half in my arms, half in my lap. I vowed two things that night: One, although I had no doubt in my mind that she could protect herself, I would never let another bad thing happen to her; and two, I would find Paul Griffith, if he was still alive, and finish what her dad had set out to do years ago.

CHAPTER 5

Summer was past its prime and school was getting ready to start all over again, bringing a close to the all too brief reprieve of responsibility. Amber and I traveled quite a bit over the summer break, hiking and camping along every trail we could find spanning Utah to California. We'd take off for the weekend after throwing darts at a map, exploring wherever the dart landed. Once the weekend wound down, we'd return home, clean our gear and decompress, take a couple days to catch up on life, then rinse and repeat. The time spent together was not only valued, but it helped us grow together as people and a couple.

During the last week of July, we were sitting down trying to plan a trip to the Moab, Utah to hike the red rocks. Slick Rock was a mountain biking mecca and known the world over for its multiple bike paths varying in difficulty. Amber and I loved to bike, but you could also hike the area and enjoy it just as much. I'd been to the area many times before, and immediately fell in love with the red rock beauty, the differentiating landscape, and the culture. The people who lived in the area seemed to have their own laid back, almost hippie-like culture that promoted the love of the outdoors and valued the human connection.

I leaned my head back, calling out to her as she fumbled through the cabinets for something in the kitchen, "Babe, when do you have that conference thing you have to do for the Natural Resources department?"

"Uh, it's the second week in August. The tenth I think... Why?" I could tell by her tone that she was more intent on finding some long lost utensil than accurately answering my question.

"I was going to try and fit one more little get away in, nothing big." The truth was that I had giving some serious thought to putting Amber on lock down; I just didn't know how exactly to propose or where I would ask her to marry me.

The facts were that we were pushing forty, and while we both held the belief that a piece of paper didn't define love, it was something I wanted to give her. The commitment of my love to her. There was nobody else I would rather spend my life with. She'd pulled a Jerry McGuire and 'completed me'. Truth be told, I'd already bought the ring a month before. I just needed to fine-tune the details and pull the trigger.

While we packed our gear and readied to leave for Moab the next morning, Amber pulled out our packs from the spare bedroom and was checking off her list of things to take. That's when I heard it.

"What. The. *Fuck*?!"

My ears perked and I leapt off the couch in a direct flight to where Amber was. I turned the corner and stumbled into the room, totally unprepared for what I was seeing. Amber had pulled both her and my packs out of the closet. As she was clearing her pack out, she tried to be sweet and clear mine out so that she could plant a surprise pair of lingerie for me to find. We had a ritual of keeping intimacy and fun part of our lives. However, it would seem that it was I who had planted the unexpected surprise for her. Amber turned towards me, her mouth agape with utter silence spilling out. Raising her tear-filled eyes to meet mine, I looked down to her hands as she slowly pushed them through the tension-filled air towards me in an offering.

"Orion, what in the actual fuck is this?" The nearly inaudible whisper stole away the silence.

I looked down at her outstretched arms, and that was when I saw it: the ring box. The one that held the engagement ring I had bought for her just a month before. I slowly reached forward and took the box from her as if it held the last remaining morsel of life itself. Falling to one knee, I thoughtfully rallied together an impromptu proposal now that my rehearsed speech was out the window.

"Amber, this isn't the way I had worked it out in my head... I know we talked about how paper doesn't mean anything and doesn't define what love is. The only problem with that is that I want the world to know my love and who it's for. I want there to be no question about who holds my heart." Pausing to collect my thoughts and remember the pieces of the engagement speech I had started to plan, I looked into her eyes. From here I could see the initial awe slowly fade as it was replaced by endearment and love. "I want to wrap you in my arms, until forever and one day. That one day will be to remember all the dreams we shared together. Through life's storms I want you to stay in my arms, until forever and one day. Amber Lockhart, will you marry me?"

By the time the last words had left my lips, her tears were freely falling. Her smile had spread across her face, and she fought to answer through the emotions. All she could do was nod. Cry, smile, and nod.

The next few hours were a blur of phone calls and celebratory announcements. She called her mom, and I called some of the guys to let them know the good news. My dad had died years back and I had no clue where my mom was, let alone talked to her since I was a teenager. I had no immediate family to tell. The first call I made was to Stew. He and I talked at least every other week and were up to speed on the ins and outs of what each other was doing. I'd mentioned that I was thinking of asking Amber to marry me when it had first come up about a month before.

"Congrats, brother! I couldn't be happier for you." I could hear him smiling through the phone. "When's the big day?"

"Bro, I just asked her. We haven't even talked about it. I'll let you know what's going on and when because I'm gonna need you to stand right by me. I want you to be my best man. What do you say?" Marcus agreed the very second the last word left my mouth. I knew he'd accept. Asking him was merely a formality.

The phone calls ended and Amber and I both collapsed on the couch; our bodies still enthralled by the high but both exhausted. There was only one thing left to do. I stood up and bent over to scoop her up in my arms. As I carried her to the bedroom, she nestled her face in the crook of my neck and gripped her arms around me a little tighter. It was time to consummate this celebratory moment.

We still had a day of travel and two days of hiking ahead of us and we both chased the excitement and lack of proper rest with coffee—cup after cup of coffee. After loading the truck with our hastily packed bags and equipment, we hit I-15 and headed south to Zion's National Park.

"Ry, where do you want to get married? I don't mean *where* like Logan-where, but say in a church or somewhere?" Her bare feet were propped up on the dash as she leaned back, allowing her to bask in the morning sun as it lit the inside of the truck.

"I don't see any reason to get married in a church. You know how I feel about organized religion, especially here in Utah. The Mormon church is a scam, under the guise of religion, to cheat people out of ten percent of their income when all it is is a membership fee to let them into their misogynistic White Kids Club temple."

Amber and I had had many many long discussions about religion, and she, for the most part, felt the same way. She didn't harbor nearly the same disdain for the local Mormon religion that I did, but she didn't take to a particular religion, and so the Mormons didn't bother her. She felt that if believing a certain way made someone happy then by all means do it.

"Oh hell, here we go again". I couldn't see her eyes roll behind her Oakleys, but I knew damn well she was doing it. "I only meant a church because it's kind of traditional. Jesus, Ry... Haha."

The woman could work me up and calm me down in a matter of seconds, and truth be told, I kind of liked it. "What about that castle-type place on the edge of town that you can rent? Castle mansion or something?"

"Yeah, that could work, but why don't we just do it outside somewhere? We could go up the canyon or you could get in touch with some of your fellow nature nerds in the department and put in some calls to the forestry service?"

A smile and her middle finger were the only response I got.

We reached Moab six hours later and checked in to the hotel. It was just after one o'clock and there was plenty of daylight left. After dropping our bags in the room, we decided to drive up to Slickrock bike trail and check out the area. The trail was only a couple of miles out of town and fairly easy to find. The parking lot was full except for one spot in the back. We grabbed our packs out of the back of the truck and took to walking the practice loop that was made up of the very first part of the trail.

The sun felt amazing as we followed the worn black rubber, single-lane path that had been worked into the rock by bikes over the years. The trail wound for miles all along the rock. Most of the area was flat, but parts of it danced along the edge of the cliffs, giving the most immaculate views to the river bed eight-hundred feet below. A few hundred yards from the entrance of the trail, Amber stopped along the edge, turning to face me. I had never seen anything or anyone so beautiful. The brightness of the sun couldn't compete with her, and it knew better than to try.

She had on a worn out ball cap of mine to keep her hair off of her neck. She took the hat off and shook her hair out in the most sexy display of flirtatious 'I know you want me, but you're gonna have to wait until we get back to the hotel' that I had ever seen. I reached for my phone to take a picture. She grinned slyly, "Oh, you want a picture, do ya?" She turned to face the miles of red rock canyon along the horizon then shuffled towards the part of the trail that overlooked the river. I raised the phone and readied to take the picture. The backdrop was perfect.

Amber turned to face me again as the smile that I had grown to love and would soon marry spread from ear to ear. "I sure love you, Amber Lockhart."

I pressed the button on my phone. *Click.*

I slid the phone back into my pocket as I started walking towards her.

"Orion, promise me that we will always continue our little adventures." She switched her hips back and forth, subtly posing for me.

"I can't think of anything I'd rather do than experience the world with you, babe."

She switched her hips again and stepped back half a step, playing 'come and get me'.

She didn't realize that she was so close to the edge.

She didn't see the loose gravel.

The last thing I remember was hearing my name as it echoed the entire eight-hundred feet to the river below.

CHAPTER 6

There isn't much left to do for a man who has lost everything. I lost my fiancée two years ago. I lost my house to memories, and I was starting to lose myself. After she died, I couldn't bear to stay there anymore. The past haunted me every second that I stayed in that house. I couldn't look at her pictures without feeling my heart stop. I would look at our bed only to feel my breath be stolen from my chest. Hell, I couldn't even make scrambled eggs without breaking down because the damn spatula we bought together would only serve to remind me of the love that was taken from me. The only thing that served purpose to justify my life was my job, and even that thread was frayed.

The funeral was a blur. Her parents had her service in Logan, Utah, where she had spent the majority of her life. It was a simple service where we memorialized her life and all that she had done during her shortened time on earth. Friends and family said some kind words or told stories; some funny, some of childhood heroics, giving light to the life that had been lost. Of the almost two-hundred people there, I had only ever met her mom and dad.

I got to the church two hours early. I had been lost since she died, and today was no different. I had been wandering through town and life with no direction. I trudged through the doors of the church and stared at the empty pews. The church was lit by the sun that shined through the stained-glass windows lining the stone walls of the church. The altar stared back at me as the cross that hung behind it loomed ominously. My head began to spin as the empty room echoed with the sounds of my memories. I could hear her voice encouraging me to "go on" and walk up to the front of the church. She had supported me in confronting my demons through life and she continued even now.

My legs felt heavy as I moved towards the front of the church. Throughout my life, I had picked up burdens—burdens I had carried to this day. The burdens of my youth. The burdens of war. The burden of taking the lives of my enemies. The burden of being forgotten by my parents and the hate and resentment that came with that. Amber knew all of this, and she knew that, partly because of this, I wasn't overly religious. She suggested that I not do it to find the "truth and light", but rather to unleash the burden. She said I should use it as a confession of sorts. She said that, by confessing my sorrows, sins, or dropping the weight that I had carried for the past twenty-plus years, I would finally be able to begin healing and moving forward with my life.

I felt that I had been moving forward; I was an accomplished soldier who had now turned toward a life of learning and was pursuing a peaceful life. I had found my soulmate.

She was the June Carter to my Johnny Cash. She knew me better than I knew myself. She would hear my mumbles and wake when I tossed and turned in bed with the nightmares that haunted my sleep. Most times, it would be the harsh memories of war that rattled me at night, but every once in a while, my childhood would come back to me in my sleep and destroy the walls I had built up, protecting me from my past. I had always brushed her off and never really taken what she said to heart. But even after her death, I could still hear her soft, melodic voice encouraging me forward.

I hadn't realized I was unconsciously moving forward toward the front of the church, but minutes later, I was standing in front of the small stage area at the bottom of two steps. My legs, heavy from emotion, lurched up the stairs as my shoes rang out the light tap on the wood beneath them. The cross, approximately fifteen feet tall, was looming over me like a lighthouse on a storm-riddled coast. My dry throat kept me from speaking even a whisper, although I really didn't know what to say. My mind that had been racing moments ago with a million thoughts was suddenly blank.

I finally found the ability to speak, but the raspy voice didn't sound like me. "Lord... Uh, whoever, I guess. Look, I don't really know how this works. I'm not sure who I'm even talking to or what I should say. I guess I'm only really doing this because of the woman I love. Amber told me that, by talking to you and confessing, I could shed some of this weight that I've carried around for so long."

My voice had found its legs and was starting to stand on its own, but I couldn't bring myself to talk louder than a whisper. I was looking at the cross and talking to it as if it were a real person and could hear me. Having slowly forgotten how crazy I felt earlier, talking to an inanimate object, I stared on in silence for minutes on end. The words came back to me and I felt myself speaking again. "I was beaten, abused, forgotten, and forsaken when I was a child. I knew the love of a belt against my back or the kiss of a hand across my face long before I knew of tenderness. I kept my rage bottled up until I joined the Army. When I joined Special Operations, I was given one job: to defeat the enemy. I was to complete that job by any means necessary. I began to use my skill set as an outlet for the anger and rage I'd kept bottled up for so long. I killed not just for my country or the safety of those around me or the innocent men, women, and children of whatever God-forsaken country I was in; I killed because I pictured my mother's face every time I squeezed the trigger. I pictured the countless beatings I'd endured from my mother's boyfriends so much that the scars throbbed.

"The recipients of my angst never knew how much I hated my mother until the bullet buried itself inside their skull. I don't regret the things I've done; I've done what I've done for the purpose of bettering humanity. But now... now they haunt me. I see their faces. I feel the trigger squeeze underneath my fingertip, and I can taste the carbon in the air. My life was miles and miles of hate and rage."

My throat had suddenly gone dry again. I could feel emotion that had for years been lost rushing to the surface with a maddening speed. I could feel my eyes begin to fill as I was able to speak again. "That was until I met Amber. I... I'd finally found my soulmate. She was an angel sent to save me when I didn't even know I needed saving. She helped me see the good in myself and never left my side... Until now.

"I don't know why you had to take the one good thing I had in my life, but damn you for doing it. I thought you were all about love and tending to your flock, but you let the best one die. You showed me— a sinner of some of the most abominable sins known to man—the greatest thing in life: love. Then, after you gave me everything, you ripped her from my arms." My hoarse whisper had now grown into a sullen rage. I could feel my muscles tense under my suit jacket. I hung my head in defeat and disgust as I slowly turned around. "You don't even exist, do you? But if you *are* real... you can go to Hell."

My shoulders slumped, and I began to shuffle to the back of the church when I heard someone lightly clear their throat. I looked up and could see a man dressed in a white robe with colored embroidery. I guessed he was the pastor of the church. He was rather short and stout with a round face. He looked to be in his late fifties or early sixties, and he had a way about him. He is what I would imagine Santa Clause to look like if Santa Clause had a reddish-brown beard and was vacationing in Utah.

I slowed my shuffle and looked him in the eyes.

"Son, are you okay?" He took a familiar tone with me, and I almost felt as if I knew him in the same way. I couldn't explain it, but the anger I had felt was no longer pulsing through me.

"I'm fine, sir. Thank you."

"Paul. Please call me Paul." When he gave his name, he smiled ever so slightly. "I couldn't help but hear your conversation. I take it you knew Amber well?" Paul invited me to sit on the last pew in the back of the church where we had met. I wasn't in the mood to talk to anyone and I had never been one to share my feelings, but Paul had something about him that immediately put me at ease.

We sat on the hard wooden bench and I put my head in my hands as they rested on my legs. Paul sat quietly on the bench, allowing me time to think and gather my thoughts.

"So, Amber was someone special to you?" He could have easily connected the dots if he had overheard anything of my argument with the cross.

"She was my girlfriend, my fiancé. Although girlfriend is hardly the word to describe what she really was. She was my everything." I had never been an open book before, and here I was spilling my deepest feelings and thoughts to a stranger that I had just met. I couldn't place it, but he seemed familiar to me. I didn't feel like he was a stranger.

"I'm not sure who you were talking to but it sounded like you were angry. You were telling someone to *go to Hell*." Paul was a prying little man.

I sat up looked at him. I wanted to grab him and shake him like a ragdoll, but when I looked into his eyes, every bit of that emotion left me. "Paul, I lost the woman I love. God doesn't exist because, if he did, he wouldn't have taken the one perfect thing on this earth." The tears in my eyes were starting to show again.

"Orion, I've known Amber for a long time. She was a beautiful woman and a very loving soul. God's plans for us aren't always the same as our plans. It's a very sad time for us on this earth who knew Amber, but God needed her for a bigger mission."

His words did nothing but deepen the chasm that had been built in my heart. "Paul, no offense, but I'm not really in the mood for the bullshit rhetoric of religion. You don't know the things I've done and seen because, if you did, you would know that I didn't deserve something so wonderful and beautiful as Amber, but for some reason the universe saw fit to let us meet. God had nothing to do with it because, if he did, if he even existed, he wouldn't be so damn cruel as to take the one good thing—the *only* thing—that was *ever* good in my life."

Paul sat quietly and listened as I laid my feelings out in the open against my norm. He didn't interrupt me and only offered warm words and support as we talked. It was during a lull in the conversation that someone came in the doors behind us. I looked at my watch and noticed that there was only thirty minutes left until the service started. Paul, not disturbing the silence with meaningless words, warmly placed his hand on my shoulder, smiled, and walked toward the back of the church. I assumed he was going to meet the others who were there for the service.

A few moments passed and I stood up to go to the restroom and splash some water on my face. When I came out of the restroom, there were almost thirty people in the church, with more streaming in. A few polite smiles and handshakes later, I was making my way to the front pews, where her mom invited me to sit with them. They considered me part of the family as it was, and insisted I sit with family for the memorial. I still felt alone in the sea of relationships that were seated in the cold, hard pews of the church.

Words. I don't remember much of the service except for words. Words and sobs. One of her aunts spoke about her life, while a pastor—who was not Paul—spoke some comforting words about life and death. I was a little surprised when the tall, skinny, forty-something pastor stood up from his seat on the side of the stage area to speak to the gathering. At first glance one would guess him to be mid-twenties and still wet behind the ears. I was expecting Paul, but as I looked around, I couldn't see him anywhere. I concluded that he may have been visiting or perhaps a friend of the family, but when I had mentioned him to Amber's mom, she told me she didn't know of any Pastor or Priest named Paul. She told me their family had been Presbyterian all their lives and never once had they ever had a Pastor by that name.

"Orion, are you okay?" Brenda, Amber's mom, looked concerned after the Paul conversation.

"Yeah, I'm okay. It's just... Well, Paul said he'd known Amber for quite some time. He talked about her like he truly knew her."

Brenda was approached by some distant family members and excused herself. I smiled and moved to a quieter part of the church near the back. There was a small classroom off of the rectory, and I ducked in for some alone time. I stared out the windows, watching the people that had once filled the church spill out into the street and begin to drive away in their cars. My mind was blurred, and I couldn't understand why Paul would tell me he knew Amber and yet her mom had no clue of who he was. If Paul had actually known her for as long, as he had led me to believe, then there is no way Brenda wouldn't have known him. Still, I couldn't shake the sense of familiarity with Paul.

I could still hear his voice softly speak the few words that he had. There was a fatherly like touch about his hand when he placed it on my shoulder just before walking away. I was lost in my thoughts and relishing the familiarity of Paul when I heard his voice coming from behind me.

"Orion, are you doing okay?" I spun around, startled at the fact I wasn't alone.

"Paul? What..." I was stammering at his interruption, but quickly gained my composure. "Paul, I talked to Brenda, Amber's mom, and she said she'd never heard of nor had her family ever known a Paul who was their Pastor. Anything you want to tell me?"

His face softened and he smiled slightly. "I knew Amber from my visits to the congregation. I wasn't a resident Pastor and would often visit this local church to help Pastor Mark, the man who spoke during the service. I'm sorry if you feel I misled you, Orion."

It wouldn't occur to me until years later that I had never once, during our entire conversation, told Paul my name, yet he had called me by name more than once.

That wouldn't be the last time that I would see Paul.

CHAPTER 7

The room spun violently as I sat up on the side of the bed. I had spent the previous night looking through the bottom of a bottle. The unwelcomed vertigo was no surprise. The room slowed enough for me to stumble to the bathroom, but never really stopped.

I found a toothbrush, not knowing if it was mine or some transient one from a one-nighter, and attempted to scrub the crust from my mouth. The kitchen was only four steps from the bathroom sink, but felt like miles. Piecing together the coffee maker, I began the day as I did every other; lying to myself that things weren't that bad so that I wouldn't rinse my mouth out with a revolver. It had been endless months of sorrow and heartache.

Death is a dirty, thieving whore who takes what she wants when she wants.

She has no agenda, nor does she care.

It's her way or no way, and that's it.

She meant everything to me. The fact she died weighs on my eternal soul. I've tried everything to dull the pain, but nothing's worked. It's almost as if the world has stopped turning—*my* world, at least.

Children don't laugh anymore and rain on a hot sidewalk no longer signals the middle of summer. The sun doesn't shine as bright and the stars have lost their twinkle.

I found a white shirt on the floor that wasn't stained from who-knows-what and a dark blue button-down hanging in the closet. My suit coat would cover them enough for me to not get the stinkeye from my coworkers. A good ol' Irish bath would cover the stale smell.

I wasted my work day away just like I had for the last few years by staring aimlessly at the computer screen as it stared back at me. I was in charge of research for a State-funded research group, and was left primarily on my own. It made it all easier to get through the day. I didn't really want to interact with anyone anyway. The minutes ticked away and eventually the clock read four. I shut down my computer, stashed my gear in my bag, and walked out of the office. The daylight was starting to give way to gray, and I felt the impending storm in my soul.

Having no one or nothing to go home to, I wandered the streets as I often did. I no longer held my head high or carried myself like I had in the military. Instead, my head hung and my feet shuffled slowly along. I ended up on some street that I didn't even know the name of and almost bumped into an old bag lady pushing a shopping cart filled with every possession in her whole world. "I'm sorry, ma'am." I mumbled, looking down.

I could hear a feral growl begin in her throat and stole a side-eyed glance to the wandering woman. "Watch it, asshole!" she barked through a three-tooth grimace. She rattled her cart towards me as if it were a saber as I looked back down to the grimy path and continued on.

My feet dragged forward for another block when I saw a short set of stairs leading down to a heavy wooden door. A small window with thin metal bars surrounding it in a tic-tac-toe pattern sat in the middle of the door, while a dimly lit green neon sign lazily advertising Heineken peered through another window to the right of the door.

It's been three years, to the day, since I last held her in my arms. This small, dank bar held the miseries of countless hearts in her bosom. The heaviness was palpable as I found my way to an empty stool at the far end of the bar. There wasn't a fight for seats. Besides the barkeep, I was one of only four people in here. There was a couple at a corner table on the far end of the bar. They were obviously fresh off the love train and couldn't keep their hands off each other. The only other patron at the bar was an older man who was slumped over on his stool, hugging a bottle of Mad Dog he'd smuggled in.

The bartender was a large man. He wasn't large like a bouncer; he was large like an Orca whale. He wore a too-tight Pink Floyd concert tee that was stained with whatever the bar spewed at him and was trying to bring back the five-o'clock shadow. Don Johnson would not be impressed.

The bartender didn't say a word, only stared expectantly at me. "Give me a whiskey, rocks". My feet reached for the ledge at the bottom of the bar and immediately slipped off due to the buildup of who-knows-what that coated it. I shot the entirety of my drink and ordered another.

I could tell the bartender didn't like his job. He grumbled something about how he should have finished school, and poured me another three-dollar glass of mind-numbing forgetfulness. I slid a twenty dollar bill to him on the bar. At least the drinks were cheap.

That's when the evil light of the outside world exploded through the door. The newcomer's silhouette barged in, giving way to the afternoon light as it pierced the heart of the sorrow that filled the room. The jukebox was just finishing a Nickleback song as the newest member of our lonely hearts troupe sauntered across the floor and fed money into the machine.

I heard the clicking of the buttons as a song was selected. The clack of heels on the floor behind me echoed loudly and, soon after, the bar stool two seats away from me slid back from the bar. The air was immediately filled by a sweet, familiar, vanilla fragrance. Silence. The bartender ignored her, but out of the corner of my eye I could see that her body language said she didn't mind.

Silence.

Then I heard it.

The opening drum rift stabbed the smoke in the room. The guitar began to waft through the air and pierce my heart like a sharp blade twisting deep within my chest. My eyes instinctively filled with the emotion I fought to keep back. The pain stained my cheeks. My body instinctively felt the ache of her loss in every fiber. I gritted my teeth and slammed my eyes shut. I tried telling myself to breathe and relax—*Just keep breathing and relax*—but it did nothing. I had no control over the violent emotional seizure that had overcome me.

The whiskey glass in my hand fell to the bar and splashed out as it rattled around and finally settled right side up.

My hands balled up in preparation to fight.

Breathe, Ry...

My mind couldn't take the overload and my body had regressed into a primitive fight mode.

. . . *Orion, relax and pull yourself together dammit.*

I was powerless.

But I didn't care.

My head rose and I forced my eyes open as I turned to see the demon that had crushed my healing heart. It was hard to see through the tears, but I could make out the blonde hair falling around a face and settling on soft shoulders. She looked right at me and I could see the deep blue of her eyes, like an ocean, gazing through me as if she were measuring my soul. The tears began to clear enough that the details of her face began to come into focus.

The guitar attempted to revive any remaining electricity and life to the still, dead air in the bar. Its angry yet mournful wail enveloped me and squeezed the air from my lungs.

"Maybe in another life, I could find you there. Pulled away before your time. I can't deal, it's so unfair".

It was the song I'd played at Amber's memorial service. I'd cried through every note as I strummed that guitar. Every night since the day we'd met, I'd played her a song. I just couldn't bring myself to say goodbye without one. And now, as a consequence, I'd grown to hate the heavy words of this song and hadn't played it since she died. Damn, I hadn't even picked up a guitar since then.

Whoever played this song tonight either has no soul and serves to punish me or is going through their own tortuous hell. Not too many people play Offspring songs anymore, let alone this one. It's anguish and somber takes what little hope one may have left and fills a heart with sorrow.

The four minutes and thirty-three seconds of dark, black misery lasted forever. I wiped my eyes and again tried to focus on the face of my demon.

"Leaving flowers on your grave shows I still care. Black roses and Hail Marys can't bring back what's taken from me".

I heard a soft, whispered sob, and knew that whoever it belonged to was crying as well. She didn't wipe the tears away as she leaned slightly towards me and whispered the next lines of the sadness serenade. "I reach to the sky and call out your name. And if I could trade... I would".

Her breath was warm against my skin as she whispered along with the words of the song. Her voice was hypnotic. It was then—at the very moment she leaned in and infected my senses with her flowered aura—that I saw her for who she really was.

It had been three years since the sweet vanilla perfume had filled the air that I breathed.

My heart skipped.

The bar around us disappeared.

No longer was the couple in the corner or the grotesquely large bartender in the room. The sounds around us became completely silent. The only sound was that of my heart pounding in my chest and her soft breath in the still room. When my eyes cleared enough to see, I saw a ghost.

I rubbed my eyes again.

My body went numb.

With one hand, I reached forward to try and stabilize my failing strength and found the slippery bar. The other hand slowly moved toward the apparition of the most beautiful woman I had ever seen. My feet scrambled to find the floor and my mouth fell open silently screaming the words that were racing through my mind.

How could I be staring her in the face if she'd died three years ago?

She reached towards me and I felt, for the first time in forever, her soft fingertips brush my unshaven face.

Her fingers were immediately wet with tears and I managed to squeak out the words, "How... Where?"

Her finger pressed against my lips and she leaned in closer to me. "There's so much that I have to tell you. I'll explain everything in time, but the only thing you need to hear right now is that I love you. I never stopped loving you. I never will, Ry."

CHAPTER 8

With a deafening echo the world around us began to come back to life. The dull chime of glasses clanking together was met with the sound of chairs sliding on wood as the couple at the table gathered themselves and left.

The smoke-filled air invaded my nostrils, awakening the senses. The bartender looked at me as if to ask if I needed a refill, but not a word was spoken. He must have become frustrated because he turned away from Amber and me, and then left before I could even think about saying anything. My mind was a mess—scrambled like overdone eggs—as I tried to collect myself in the surroundings.

I once again looked to Amber and blinked over and over, waiting for her to vanish like smoke; to disappear into the stale air of the bar. Her warm smile filled every crack in my heart, every crevice of my soul. Her touch, surreal as it was, grounded me to the world around us. As the song faded out and came to an end, the jukebox seemingly retired and the bar lay quiet again.

The faint sound of the streets outside teased my ears. I don't remember leaving the bar, but had somehow wound up on the curb of the street, looking up at the moon as it peered through the alley and tall buildings, giving faint light to the melancholy street below. I reached down to grab Amber's hand in instinct, but felt nothing.

Empty air.

My confusion quickly gave to fear as I spun around to find her. Did she follow me out? Had I dreamt the whole thing?

Elegantly gliding up the stairs, wrapping a scarf around her slim neck, she turned her eyes up and met mine. She began smiling when a small chuckle escaped her throat. "Did you honestly think I'd left you again, babe? Don't worry... Those days are long gone. You're stuck with me forever now."

The cold air, mixed with the outside world slapping me to life, must've awoken my vocal chords as I was finally able to form a complete sentence.

"Amber, please tell me this is real. Please tell me I'm not dreaming and you're not going to vanish into thin air."

The obvious desperation and fear must have shown more than I intended as Amber pulled her hands from her pockets and once again cradled my face. "Orion, love, you don't need to worry anymore. There will never be another day that you won't see my face. Let's go back to your apartment and I'll explain everything to you there."

During the cab ride to my apartment, not another word was said. I held on to her tightly, afraid let go. The city lights flashed by us as the cab wound through the maze of streets. I never thought about how Amber knew I had sold the house and downsized to an apartment. I'd done it about a month after her memorial service. I couldn't bear living among the memories and constant reminders. The thought wouldn't cross my mind until much later that night.

Everything I thought I knew about life had just been thrown out of life's proverbial window. My dead girlfriend—the one I saw fall 1,400 feet; the one I'd had to identify for the coroner, the one I'd buried—was back in town. I didn't know what to think anymore. What else did I not know about life?

I dug my apartment keys out of my pocket and held the door open. She leaned in and lightly kissed my cheek as she passed by, stoking the fire that had exploded within me. She smoothly strode to the kitchen and grabbed a glass from the cabinet. She reached into an adjacent cabinet and took the sole occupant from the shelf, a half-empty bottle of Jack, and smoothly allowed it to spill into the glass. She brought it over and pushed it through the air to me with instructions as if it were medicine. "Here, Ry, this'll help." Her soft fingers grazed mine as I took the glass from her.

"Babe, I don't think I need any more alcohol. Besides, I have a million questions. I need..." She abruptly cut me off. "Orion, drink it. You're going to need it."

I gave in to her insistent pressure and drank the contents of the glass in one throw. She immediately took the glass from me and returned to the kitchen for a refill. "Are you trying to get me drunk? What are you *doing*?" Was my dead girlfriend trying to kill *me* now?

"You need to trust me," she instructed, her back to me as she finished pouring another drink, this one a little more than the last. "Besides, it's not like you to turn down whiskey." I saw the old familiar smile creep to her lips as she brought me the second glass of Jack.

"I trust you... That's not the issue here. And what do you mean *I'm going to need it*?"

"Ry, you need to sit down. It's time I fill you in on some things."

"Yeah, you fucking think? You died! I watched you fall. I was at your memorial service and saw you lowered into the ground. I've lived the last three years mourning you and struggling to survive, barely able to keep myself from suck-starting a shotgun." The emotions began to overtake me. I could sense the sadness, the elation of having her back, with all of the feelings blanketed by anger and complete confusion.

"About that... Thank you. I can't imagine how hard it was to sing at the service, let alone sing the song you did. It was beautiful, Ry." Her eyes softened even more and her hand reached for mine.

"Wait, how did you—" I could feel my face twist furiously as she pressed her finger to my lips, silencing the raging confusion.

My head fell back hard, resting on the cushion as I fell to the couch. I finished the last of the whiskey in my glass and set it down on the coffee table. Her long, elegant fingers reached for my chin and pressed softly into the soft spot just underneath as she turned my head towards her.

"Orion, what I'm about to tell you will take some time. I need you to listen and not interrupt. If you do that, I promise that, in time, all of your questions you have will be answered. Do you understand?"

I realized just how much I had missed her soft, piercing blue eyes as she waited for an answer. The same eyes I saw every time I closed mine.

My chest heaved and a forceful sigh escaped me. "Amber, I—"

"Orion Thorrsen, do you understand?" Her tone had become stern and the smile had fallen from her face. I knew she was serious.

"I trust you. I understand."

Her face softened slightly as she closed her eyes for a brief moment, took a deep breath in, and began. "Orion, three years ago, when I fell off Angel's Landing, I died. You saw my body on the rocks. All of it was real. But, when I was falling, something happened. I remember slipping on the gravel. I remember reaching out to you as I fell backwards into the open..."

My heart began racing as I relived each and every aspect of her death as she described it to me. I hadn't realized that where my hand had rested on her thigh had begun to firmly grip, although she showed no sign of feeling it.

"I can remember watching the ledge quickly fall away as I flailed through the air for what seemed like an eternity." She paused, gathering herself again before continuing. "I could see the ledge getting further and further away, and I knew that, any second, I'd hit the rocks below. But I never did."

I could tell she saw the bewilderment on my face, and yet the corner of her mouth curled upward, ever so slightly.

"The next thing I remember after falling was a complete warmth washing over me and a blinding light. The light was so bright that I had to close my eyes, but it didn't do anything to help. Even with my eyes shut I could still feel the invading light. The feeling of falling had stopped, and it was as if I was being carried. I felt the arms of someone underneath me, carrying me like a child. The light began to soften and, when I was finally able to open my eyes, all I could see was white. An enormous wall of white feathers around me like curtains blocking out the world. The feathers moved and shifted individually, but they were all a part of something bigger. I followed them and began to make out wings. The wings slowly opened up and I found myself in the most beautiful room. The walls were lined with books that sat on ornate wood shelves. There were thousands and thousands of books. There were stairs that led to more levels above, and there I saw more shelves with different books and, above that, more of the same. I found my feet and stood up as whoever was holding me set me down. I was more than confused. One minute I was falling and then next... Well, I found myself standing in the most elaborate, beautiful library I've ever seen. I hadn't seen who'd carried me there, let alone known exactly how I got there. I probably should have been scared given that I was falling over a thousand feet one second and the next being held in a stranger's arms like an injured, helpless animal... but I wasn't."

As she began telling me the next part of her experience, her face lit up. There was a beautiful, loving glow that overcame her, and her voice cracked slightly as she almost cried as the words began to spill from her mouth.

"I turned to see who had carried me and where exactly the wings led to or from. That's when I first came face to face with Gabriel."

"Gabriel?" I wasn't asking from a place of jealousy and Amber could see that.

"Yes, Gabriel. *The* Arch Angel Gabriel. I instinctively stepped back to take everything in, and that's when I saw his wings fully open, spread wide.

They were beautiful. They were whiter than anything I've ever seen, and I could immediately feel their power. Gabriel stood tall and didn't say a word as I looked him over, turning back to the library, and again back to him. He spoke, and when he did, I couldn't help myself from crying. His voice was the most beautiful sound I'd ever heard.

"'Amber Lockhart, I am Gabriel. Everything will be explained in time, but right now you are in The Great Hall. The books you see before you hold the deeds of every person who has ever lived. Each person has their own book and every action, whether good or bad, is recorded in their book. The reason I've brought you here is three fold.'

"I'll honestly never forget any of his words..."

Amber closed her eyes as if she were taking in the sights and sounds of that moment all over again. "Orion, I couldn't speak. I wanted to, of course, but I couldn't bring my body to make a sound, or even string words together in a sentence. I tried to compose myself and gather what little strength I could, but before I could force even a squeak from my lips, Gabriel had answered the lingering question for me.

"'Yes, Amber, you are dead. Your body is now lay on the rocks below the ledge from which you fell. What you see and feel right now is your soul. Your soul feels physically like your body did on Earth, but as you will find, it is vastly different. Now, as I mentioned, there are three main reasons you are here with me in The Great Hall. The first is that the life that you lived on Earth has earned you a place in Heaven. The second is that we are asking you to fulfill a calling; we would like you to be a guardian angel.'

"You can imagine how surreal that was..."

Amber was explaining what had happened in such a matter-of-fact way that I was convinced it had actually happened, but at the same time I thought she was absolutely insane. Wings, The Great Hall, Gabriel, the Arch Angel. It was all so farfetched, but so was the fact that she was even sitting next to me on my couch at that very moment.

"I finally found my voice and asked him what that meant exactly—to be a guardian angel, I mean. And he told me that I would come to know all that being a guardian angel entails, but that it was more or less just what humans think it is. He told me I'd be assigned a soul—what they call humans on Earth—and that I would guide them according to their plan. He told me, if they were to deviate from their path in such a way that it could alter their future from the plan or even alter the future of others, it would be up to me, the guardian, to intervene.

"'No one will be able to see you and you are to do all your work in a "behind the curtain" manner', he said to me. 'Each and every person has been assigned a guardian angel.' That's when I asked Gabriel if he was *my* guardian angel. I mean, he'd taken me away from my fall, and one could assume that he'd been looking over me. That's when he explained that he wasn't my guardian angel at all, but that he'd been asked to intervene. And that was when he told me the third reason I was standing in The Great Hall...

"'Amber, you've earned your place in Heaven, and we are asking you to be a guardian angel. There is another, far greater reason that you are here, however. Once you have gone through your initiatory period and received your instructions on being a guardian, we'll need you to recruit another soul to a higher calling. Much like the stories that have been told for thousands of years, there is a war in Heaven that has been fought since the beginning of time, but things have changed and the enemy has escalated his tactics and taken the war beyond the people of Earth'."

I was starting to think Amber had lost her mind, but then quickly thought the same of myself.

I couldn't quite wrap my head around everything that was happening. I also couldn't shake the nagging that I had started to feel deep inside me, begging me to recognize it. "Amber, who did Gabriel say the enemy was?" *What the hell? Was I really buying this?*

"Orion, I think you already know who. Lucifer. Gabriel said he goes by Luc, keeping with the times and all. Even though the world has progressed—or digressed, depending on your point of view—Lucifer couldn't get away with using his full name and was still forced to hide in plain sight among the living. Gabriel went on about the increased threat to the world and that the Arch Angels were being hunted like prey." Genuine concern and sadness blanketed her face as she talked about Lucifer, or Luc as he was now known.

"Okay, so it's no surprise that you punched your ticket to Heaven, Amber. Anybody who knows you knows you're worthy. The fact you were called to be a guardian angel isn't too far out of reach either. I imagine you have to be pretty pure to be asked to look over a human being. The last thing, though... Did he say who you were supposed to recruit?"

Amber didn't have to answer. It was written all over her face. The sadness was replaced by a smile, and I could feel her warmth deep within my chest. Without saying a word, she had confirmed the answer to my question. The warmth in my chest grew until it fully took over me.

"Wait, what the... Whoa, *no*! Amber, what the hell?!" I tried jerking my hand away from hers as the confusion quickly spread to fear and panic deep within me. I started to get up from the couch, but Amber's hand onto mine tightly. Almost immediately, the panic and fear began to subside, and the warmth I felt earlier began to return.

"Ry, do you trust me?" The rhetorical question needed no answer, yet she waited patiently for one.

"Of course I do, Amber. It's just that... You... This ... and now *this*? What the hell am I supposed to think?" I took a minute to gather my thoughts and to enjoy the warmth filling the last of the voids within me. "So, you mean to tell me that *you* were sent to recruit *me* to be a guardian angel?" Hearing myself say the words forced me to come to terms with them, but it didn't change the fact that I felt batshit crazy for letting them slip out.

"No, I'm not the one that will recruit you. I'm only here to set up the meeting. I've been sent to *assist* in the matter, if you will," she said with a smile. "If you agree, I'll take you to the place where you'll meet with someone who'll answer every question and make the calling official by offering it to you."

"Amber, there's one minor detail I want to point out and that's the fact that I'm *not dead*. Isn't that kind of obvious?"

She laughed, and I realized just how much I had missed that melodic sound. "You're not" She laughed again. "Look, I know that this is a *lot* to take in. Believe me, I know. This whole night has got to be mind-blowing, but I promise this is only the beginning. If you agree to go with me, I can guarantee two things. Shit will get strangely weird, one. And two, you will realize exactly why you've become the person you are today. All the pain, all the trials you've endured in life—your childhood, your service, everything. It will all make sense."

It didn't take a mad scientist to know: I had nothing to lose. I had Amber back, in whatever capacity that was. The only issue was that it was in my nature to know everything about the mission. Every little detail. But something told me this mission was far bigger than myself or than simply taking out a single target.

I saw the gravity of the question in her eyes and, without consciously deciding to, I nodded my head. "As long as I get to keep you, I'm in."

"Orion, you don't know how important the decision you have just made truly is..."

Yeah, no shit because I knew nothing *of what I'd agreed to.*

"Alright, shall we?" Amber stood up and reached her hand down to help me up. "We really need to get going."

"In the words of Letterkenny Wayne, 'pitter-patter, let's get at 'er'." The sarcasm involuntarily bled from me. "So, now what?" The question was left unanswered as Amber stood before me and raised her right hand, covering my eyes. Her soft touch was all I wanted, and the feelings rushed through me like a raging river.

"Ascend." This one word, whispered from her lips, fleeced my ears as the unseen world around me violently shook. A blinding light thrust through the spaces between her fingers and stabbed at my closed eyelids.

The floor of the apartment began to shake. And that's when I felt it.

Pain.

An immeasurable weight jetted through my heart. The sensation was so powerful it rendered me speechless. I couldn't even scream, try as I might. I tried to reach out to hold on to Amber, to steady myself, to do something, but it was so much I couldn't move a muscle. I could feel every cell in my body begin to shake and, within seconds, they felt as if they were set on fire. My ears were filled with the most hellish, rumbling sound as if a thousand trains were all blowing their whistles at once, right in the middle of my head. I could feel the noise in my spine.

The blinding light poured through my closed eyes like molten metal. The weight overcame me. Any second now I would be crushed by the invisible liquidator.

It was death. And I was dying.

CHAPTER 9

Silence.

There was no sound. My eyes no longer felt the searing pain or the bright light that had scorched through my eyelids. My hands, still clenched to my chest, began to once again feel the flow of blood as they relaxed. I must have fallen down after Amber put her hand over my eyes. Curled in the fetal position, I slowly extended my legs. There was no pain. There was no deafening sound. The only thing I did notice was the smell. I could smell... paper.

Paper and dust.

The kind of dust and paper smell that reminded you of boxes and boxes of books as the pages were fanned in front of your face. If this was a Victoria's Secret perfume, it would be called 'Rustic Library'.

That's when I heard her.

"Ry, it's over now. It's going to be okay." My ears echoed with her soft, soothing voice above me. I didn't feel as if my ears were profusely bleeding. Kneeling beside me, her hand rested on my arm as I resisted fear and cautiously opened my eyes. Soft light peeked back at me as I blinked several times to get used to my surroundings. Slowly I got up and took in my environment.

I was standing in The Great Hall.

"Amber, are we... Are we in The Great Hall?" My voice felt distant and my throat dry and raspy. It seemed like a rhetorical question, but no other words came to me.

"Yes, Ry. That's exactly where we are. How do you feel?" She turned to stand in front of me as I stood erect, placing both of her hands on my arms in a steadying manner.

"What was that? What happened?"

"Orion, you had to go through physical death. I neglected to mention that when I told you about what happened with me."

"Yeah, you could have at least given me the heads up. Next time, eh?" Instinctively reaching for my neck to rub out the soreness and tension, I stopped short and noticed there was none. Everything I had felt was as if it had never happened.

"I've never seen death from this point of view. I remember my own, but it was almost as painful to watch. The sounds, the screaming... I could feel the torment and pain emanating from you, from your soul."

I could feel the sympathy in her voice. There seemed to be a little bit of pain in there, too.

"You, you put your hand over my eyes and the next thing I knew my eyes were being stabbed by light, and my body went rigid." I began an overall self-check as I patted myself down from head to toe. Nothing felt out of place, and I didn't notice any soreness or pain whatsoever.

Registering my confusion, she filled me in. "You don't feel pain anymore. Ever. It's a perk of the job." Her wink at the end made me smile. I straightened myself and stood tall, looking upwards to the ceiling. The place was massive.

As I turned around and around, craning my head upwards at the seemingly endless levels and shelves of books, I indirectly questioned her, "So what happens now?"

Just as I spoke the last syllable, I heard what sounded like a large door closing in a distant alcove. I didn't hear footsteps or any other humanly noises, like someone clearing their throat, but when I had finished my most recent pirouette, I saw him. As I leveled my eyes to meet his, the air filled with a raucous *whoosh* as the most glorious and full wings opened in a feathered applause.

He was as tall as I was. His dark brown hair loosely flowed just past his shoulders. He wore what appeared to be modern clothes; loose-fitting linen beach pants and a medieval-style shirt that hung loosely on his well-formed torso. He appeared to inconspicuously size me up before he spoke.

"Orion, my name is Michael. I asked Amber to assist in the matter and recruit you. As I'm sure she told you, there is a great war that has been fought for thousands of years. Recently, Lucifer has increased his efforts and is now threatening the immortal guardians and the Arch Angels themselves." He stood tall and firm as he spoke. He didn't appear to even blink, and he spoke wielding confidence. He then turned and motioned for me to follow him through the massive opening that I had now noticed at the very center of the room.

"Orion, it was always the plan to recruit you to be a Guardian but, until now, it was thought that you would be able to stay the course and live out many more years of your life on Earth before being called. But, as I mentioned, times have changed. The war has changed and we—much like Lucifer has done—must step up our efforts."

Michael continued talking as he turned towards the table at the center of the room, motioning for us to follow him. I soaked in every word, still confused, trying to wrap my head around the whole situation. I turned just enough to see Amber walking behind us, admiring the rows and rows of books before seeing me and smiling.

"Michael, I... I don't know what to say. I mean, I agreed to this, but I don't get why I'm any different to anybody else that has been or could have been called to be a Guardian."

By the time I finished my statement, we had moved to the center of the room. We stood in front of a large, ornate, round, wooden desk. The sides were adorned with carvings of angels, but not the Valentine's Day cherubs-in-diapers type of angels. Instead, they looked like a Marine Recon platoon full of stoic, Greek God, marble-sculpted warriors. The dark wood was smooth and glossed under the light in the room that had to be natural because I couldn't find one single light fixture anywhere. In the very center of the table was a grand book that sat closed. There was no dust anywhere on the book, yet it looked ancient. Leather-bound and approximately eight inches thick, the open edge was sealed with worn brass clasps that over-latched on the front of the book. The clasp, where a lock should be, sat bare.

"Orion, there is a lot that you must learn, and most of it you will come to know soon. First, you must be assigned a soul. Open the book and learn the name of the Earthly soul you will look after." This was the angelic, heavenly version of *shut the fuck up and know your role*, but without the arrogance. Michael was direct and to the point when he talked, with very little humor or idle talk.

With that, Michael motioned his arm outward and toward the book in the center of the table.

I reached for the book, expecting the clasp to be stuck and difficult to open. It flipped open easily, without any effort at all, but the cover was heavy as the taught leather resisted. As I opened the book and feathered through the pages, I didn't see any writing. No words, no letters. Not even a single page number. There were only blank pages.

"Michael, you uh... You want me to fill in a random name or what? There's nothing." Just then, I saw a fleeting letter on one of the pages I had flipped past. Turning back to where I had seen the lettering, I found, in the middle of the book, a single name. The first name was on the left page with the last name on the right. If I had a beating heart, it would have stopped. Somehow, I still felt the pang of shock in my chest.

"You're fucking kidding me, right?" I immediately regretted my choice of words. "Sorry, what I meant was, uh... Is this some kind of joke?" Amber hung her head to hide her smirk.

"No, Orion, this isn't a joke, and no one is *fucking kidding you*. Yes, we have a sense of humor, but not with things like this. Also, easy on the language while in the celestial world. We run by a similar set of rules as Earth and realize that the Guardians that are recruited come from all walks of life, but up here"—he looked around and motioned to the vastness of The Great Hall before looking back to me—"try and remember that this *is* an extension of Heaven. Besides, Father would not be too pleased." Michael winked as a smirk slid across his lips, leaning in just enough to get the point across to me.

It was the most polite ass-chewing I had ever had, but the fact it was given by *the* Arch Angel Michael gave it all the gravity I needed to understand. "Roger that." Sheepishly looking back to the book, I read the small, cursive print over and over. Two words. One name. a lifetime of experiences and a world of pain, heartbreak, being let down, and yet the very first person to teach me just what love was.

Lynn Sutton. It was my mother's name.

I was being assigned to guard my mother. Someone I hadn't talked to in more than fifteen years. The woman who had abandoned me and left me to fight the world on my own at just sixteen years of age. The woman who I had watched get beaten yet also drive away, never turning away to wave goodbye.

"Michael, I'm not sure about this. I don't have to explain to you my past and the childhood I had. I know you know all about it, but asking me to guard my own mother, knowing everything that happened, seems to be asking a lot." Turning my gaze from the book to Amber and then back to Michael, I saw concern. Amber looked worried, but she knew how difficult my childhood had been. I had told her all about the hell I had endured and how much disdain I had for my mother. Michael's face was harder to read, but I could still make out something. His slightly wrinkled forehead and sad eyes led me to think he was drawing on my history as well, but more than that, it was as if I could feel him in my heart, rummaging around and drowning in the sorrow, the pain, and the fear.

"Orion, I'm not quite sure why our Father chooses the souls he does. I don't question it, nobody does, but he has a reason for everything. Perhaps he wants you and your mother to reconnect. Maybe she's in great danger and he knows that, even though you endured the childhood you did, you are the only one that can protect her with all of your heart and keep her from any plot Lucifer may have."

The immediate concern must have flashed on my face. "Why would Lucifer be concerned with my mom? Some broken, alcoholic woman who life has ridden hard and put away wet..."

"Orion, Lucifer has stepped up his game. He is using tactics that would have been seen as quite egregious or out of line a millennia ago. He isn't just targeting the souls on Earth. He's gone after Celestial beings. He has tried targeting us directly. By using his demons to try to kill us, but they are no match for us. Demons are his tools for souls on earth. They are the whispers of evil thoughts in the ears of humans. The bad ideas and horrific actions that happen between souls are, most of the time, the result of a demon's influence on that soul or souls.

"Lucifer knows he can't win this war by using the souls of Earth alone. He's starting to target us himself. Sometimes he tries to get to those on Earth in order to sway us from our duties or deter us from protecting the population of souls. Our brother Raphael, one of the seven Arch Angels, returned to Celestia. He was murdered on Earth as he protected a soul who was to be called as a guardian." Michael reverently bowed his head, paying homage to his brother. Still looking down to the marble floor of The Great Hall, Michael continued softly, "The only person that can kill an Arch Angel—or *any* angel for that matter—is another angel. Lucifer's demons don't have the power or abilities to harm us, but Lucifer... Well, Lucifer was an angel until he fell. He's the only one that could have challenged or killed Raphael." His head still hanging low, Michael's somber seemed to emanate through the hall.

"Michael, wait... Are you telling me the demons of Hell are stepping up their game of evil on Earth, but that Lucifer himself is coming after the Arch Angels directly? You're saying Lucifer has *killed the* Arch Angel Raphael and that Armageddon is knocking on the door with a twenty-pound sledge hammer?" My years of disbelief or doubt in anything related to God or a higher power seemed to dissipate immediately, given the fact I was now standing in the Great Hall that, apparently was centered in Celestia, or what I understood to be Heaven.

His head slowly raised as our eyes met. I could still feel the melancholy of the moment, but something else, too. I could feel rage. Michael didn't show it, of course, but a man who has served his country and fought as I have knows when the man across from him is feeling rage. Michael was brimming with it.

He kept his composure as he answered me. "That's exactly what I'm saying, Orion. Lucifer is hell-bent on the fall of mankind in a sinister, backwards revenge plot against Father. He intends to bring the end of times full circle—and he intends to do it soon."

This was a lot to take in. I looked off behind Michael and to the books that lined the shelves. Without saying a word, I turned to Amber. Her reassuring smile and soft glow gleaned back at me.

It had been years since I had fought for a cause, but I couldn't think of a more worthy one than this. I felt a burning as the pilot light to my soul exploded. This is what I was born to do.

"Michael, I'm in."

CHAPTER 10

There's no Guardian Angel training center or a step program for promotion. There're a few guidelines that are shared with you, but other than that they let you off the leash. Michael said it was your past, your experiences, that they rely on when it comes to you doing what they ask you to do.

Not everyone is recruited to be a guardian, of course. Sure, everyone has the chance to go to Celestia when they die, but not everyone has what it takes to be a protector, to be a Guardian.

Michael broke this down for me and gave me a few tips and pointers before telling me to "Go and do, Orion." If I'm being honest, I have no idea what in the actual fu... I've got no idea what I'm doing. I just know I'm supposed to guide Lynn, my mom, through life. Apparently, I'm not supposed to get directly involved in her life; in other words, I'm not supposed to stand in front of a train and stop it if she gets stuck on the tracks. No, it works a little differently than that. Instead of altering the immediate reality, I'm supposed to just guide and *suggest* alternate courses as she goes through life. I can't just David Blaine myself from a cloud of smoke—*poof!*—and tell her not to take the second-left off of Center Street because the Meadow Gold Dairy truck is going to broadside her. No. Everything I do is supposed to be from behind the curtain, so to speak.

Now do something for me a second. Picture a loved one you've lost and something you see from time to time or in everyday life that reminds you of them. It could be a butterfly, an eagle soaring overhead, a certain song. That's how we're supposed to let you know we're there. Those things that people think are signs are exactly that. Sometimes it's warranted that we show ourselves or intervene directly, but those times are rare and reserved for extreme cases.

Another thing that is different to life is that Guardians don't sleep. We don't need it. We don't get tired. Now, we can lie down, close our eyes and relax, but it's not necessary or vital to our existence. We also don't need to eat. We can and sometimes do, though. Let me be honest: if I couldn't ever have Ben & Jerry's Karmel Sutra ice cream again, or if I couldn't ever enjoy a tall, cold pint of beer again, I wouldn't call that Celestia. I'd call it Hell.

As for getting around, it's just like you'd expect it to be. We can show up anywhere and at anytime. We don't have to take trains, planes, or any other transportation, but we can and often do. It's all part of watching over our Soul. If they take the subway, for instance, we usually would, too. And with that said, it's not uncommon to see other Guardians as we go about our daily lives. We aren't with our Souls every minute, but we see each other more times than not. That's another thing... Children. They can sometimes see us. Babies can *always* see us, but as a child gets older, they seem to lose that connection to the other side; that closeness. Not all of them lose it, but most do.

After the few pearls of wisdom that Michael bestowed upon me, he bid me farewell and said he would be checking in on me from time to time. If I had any questions, I was to use my best judgement. He said the last part and kept his gaze on me for a few extra seconds. It was an unspoken, "Watch yourself and don't do dumb shit" kind of look, not all too different to the one your father would give if he were lecturing you before you head out of town for the weekend.

After Michael disappeared, Amber gave me a little pep talk. "Ry, you'll be fine. As far as what to do, just look at it like you're protecting a high-value target from the enemy. You're a natural protector." Her voice hadn't lost its effect; it had always calmed me and apparently still did. "As for your mom, whether you believe it or not, who is there better to watch over her? I know your past was torture. And I imagine this might be overwhelming, having not seen her for almost twenty years, but you still care about her and I know you still love her. Deep down"—Amber placed her hand on my chest, and I could feel her warmth through my clothes—"you love her more than you're willing to admit."

I disagreed, but it was more out of my habitual feelings that I had experienced while alive.

I hadn't thought to ask Michael how to find out where my mom was living now. "Amber, so... how do I find my mom? It's not like I can jump on Facebook and look her up." My sneering lip curled up with my attempt at sarcasm. I really just wanted to learn a cool Angel trick.

"Why can't you, Ry? That's exactly how *we* find people. The internet is a very useful tool, even for angels." Her thin, brown eyebrow raised on one side in her 'you think you're so funny' look. With her arms folded across her chest, she waited for my response. "Wait a minute. You mean to tell me that, in order for a Celestial being—an angel, a Guardian, no less—to find someone, we have to use the *internet*?" Disbelief poured from my voice. "What, is there some sort of database you use to look up someone's name and address? Let me guess, you call it *The Cloud...*"

Amber's lips parted, her beautiful smile lighting her up like the angel she always has been—yep, I said it. A small laugh escaped her throat. "Ry, are you kidding me? Do you really think we'd rely on a man-made invention in order to track the souls of

Earth?" Her eyes rolled sarcastically as she hit my shoulder in a playful jab.

"Alright, alright. Cut the crap. So, how do I find her?"

"All you have to do is focus on her. When Michael was talking in the Great Hall, did you feel the mood change? When he talked about Raphael, could you feel the whole room grow kind of *sad*?"

I knew I had felt it, but I'd just figured it was a human emotional response based on the situation. "Well, yeah. I felt it. I mean, it was sad and a little scary to think Lucifer is targeting Angels now."

"Ry, Michael reached out to you in order to connect with you. It's like an invisible tether to your heart. He wanted you to feel the emotion so he could convey the gravity of the situation we're up against. Angels do the same thing with the souls they guard. You reach out and connect to them. When you do, you can pinpoint where they are and then you're off."

"So, I just try and focus on someone and I can control their moods and emotions, in addition to finding them?" As I said this, I tried to focus on Amber. I wanted to control the mood between us, to try out my new power. I tried concentrating on her, connecting to her heart in a metaphysical way, but nothing seemed to be happening. The mood of the room wasn't changing. I closed my eyes and tried concentrating even harder, but still nothing.

Opening my eyes, I saw Amber staring impatiently at me, toes tapping.

"Ry, you're such a guy still. Look, it doesn't work between us. The only ones that can influence an angel is an Arch. Guardians can influence souls. It's a hierarchy kind of power. So, try it again. Focus on your mom. Just think of her... And what I mean is, think of her with your *heart*."

I closed my eyes and tried. I didn't know if I needed to close my eyes, but being new at it all, I thought it best to fully concentrate.

Amber's soft voice continued, "Okay. Try and reach out to her with emotion, your heart connecting to hers."

I concentrated on a memory of my mom from when I was about six or seven years old. She was standing in the kitchen making chocolate chip cookies. It was around Christmas time. I could see her bleached blond hair falling out of the hair clip, framing her face. That's when I felt the warmth of her smile. It was more than the memory. It was an actual warmth I felt surging through me. It pinpointed directly to my heart—well, where my heart *should* be. My eyes sprang open to find Amber smiling again.

"There you go, Orion. That's it. Now, all you have to do is imagine yourself tethered to her." As Amber spoke, she reached out to my arm and gripped it securely. In what was a moment so quick that it was immeasurable, we were standing at the end of a street lined with quaint cottage-type houses. Amber released her grip on my arm. "Orion, you did it. I don't have the memories of your mom and that's why I held on to you. I could have found her by working my way through other Souls, but it was easier just to piggy back off of you."

I looked around, still astonished that I had just teleported from Celestia to this quiet street that looked somewhat familiar. "Amber, are we..." It looked just like a small street in my hometown.

"Yes, Orion. We are in Logan. Your mom moved back a few years ago and, in fact, lives quite close to where you used to. I kept tabs on her from her last Guardian, Brett. Listen, babe, I've got to go check in on my Soul. Why don't you go and take a look and pay her a visit while you figure this whole Guardian thing out, okay?" And with a wink, she was gone—like a wisp into thin air. No vapor trail, no smoke. Gone.

Shaking my head with a lighthearted smile to Amber, I looked down the street at the row of houses. I found myself walking down Marindale Avenue. Her house was nestled between two others with similar small yards. The white paint was chipping and, as I got closer, I could see the shiplap siding crumbling on the corners from years of weather and water damage. The narrow street, all of the houses sandwiched on it, and the mature tree overgrowth, gave it the small-town neighborhood feeling. If you had grown up in the 1950s, it was here, on this street.

A random dog barked as I approached the front porch. Slowly climbing up the worn steps, I could see her through the sheer curtains that hung limp in the windows. She was rummaging through the kitchen, clearly looking for something. With a quick tightening of my muscles, lasting only as long as the beat of a human heart, I pushed through the wall to the living room inside. Stealthily moving to the kitchen, I peeked around the corner—and there I could see all of her.

Time had taken its toll on my mother. Her once-smooth, California-tanned face was leathered and wrinkled. She used to look so much younger than her age and people would often tell her so. Now, she looked all of her seventy-two years—and then some.

I half-hid behind the wall until she quickly stood up and looked in my direction. She began walking towards me when I felt a pull as she walked right through me. She didn't see me, but I could feel her walk through me. I figured she hadn't felt anything until I turned around to see her shiver for a brief second as she reached for her glass on the coffee table. It was ten-thirty in the morning, but she was already on her second helping of wine. It was her classic go-to wine, Franzia in a box. The classy stuff.

Some things never change, I thought.

With purpose, she marched back into the kitchen, opened the fridge, and hastily filled her glass with fermented grapes. It had been over fifteen years, but it seemed that very little was different. Before our falling out, she had married, but I had had very little to do with him. He seemed nice enough; I mean, he didn't beat her like the last three guys she'd been with before him. I hadn't seen him since then, either, not until I heard a rustling in the back bedroom. Sidestepping through the hallway, I peeked in to the bedroom and saw that he, too, had become a victim to the curse of time.

Well before I was recruited to Celestia and before I had fallen into the darkness of depression, I had worked out daily. I would see eighty-year olds in the gym exercising and at least staying active. But these two clearly hadn't taken the initiative to stay young—and, in fact, had let time steal their youth without so much as putting up a fight.

With her wine in-hand, my mom fell onto the couch and instinctively reached for the TV remote. She punched the channel button, aimlessly surfing through daytime TV. She settled on what seemed to be a Hallmark-esque movie as the remote fell from her hand and she raised the glass to her lips. The movie was about a young boy who was being bullied at school. He would come home only to be neglected by his mother. The father didn't seem to be in the picture. How ironic that she would settle on *that* show with this being my first day on the job.

I turned from the television and studied her face. I could see her smile from years ago; I could see it through the wrinkles and sadness she now wore. I could see the crows' feet fall from the outer corner of her eyes and settle on her check bones. She couldn't weigh more than a hundred and ten pounds now; she'd been a healthy one-seventy back in the day. She was tall for a woman—five-ten—and her body was proportionate. Now, when she stood, it looked as if she had lost six inches. Her back bent forward, hunching her once-tall frame. She didn't move quickly. Her steps were cautious and seemed unstable, as if she would tumble and shatter with one wrong move.

I wasn't exactly sure just how much a Soul was aware of us Guardians. I shrugged my shoulders and decided to try to find out. I searched for my voice, but it seemed to be buried in some deep, dark chasm inside me.

Eventually managing to clear my throat, I mustered a raspy whisper. "Hey, Mom." Words I hadn't muttered in years seemed foreign as they left my lips.

Nothing. She didn't flinch.

"I've missed you, Lynn." I watched as she stared blankly at the people on the screen.

I wasn't exactly sure just how much time had passed while I stood staring at her. I had moved to a small chair near the couch. I studied her. The years flew through my memories as she passed the time, oblivious to my presence. Her husband, Floyd, came in and out of the room off and on, carrying on about nothing and mumbling as he ambled from room to room. As I watched her, living out the past over and over inside my head, I could feel my heart swell. The emotions were fighting a battle inside of me; love, hate, abandonment, forgiveness, and sorrow tumbled over and over.

The show had ended and another played without her so much as flinching. Her only movements came as she sipped her Franzia from the cheap glass she held in her hand. It was when the next show started that I noticed the only change in what must have been hours. The voices on the screen played out a scene of a woman talking with a small child. The woman was instructing the child to get ready for bed as the child pled for just a few more minutes.

"Sweetheart, you need your sleep, it's late. Now, if you hurry and get your jammies on, I'll read you a story."

The child groaned for a brief second, but eventually changed and climbed into his bed. The woman had retrieved a book from somewhere in the house and sat down on the bed to begin reading. As she read the story, the feelings in my heart began to calm, and I could feel a sense of warmth—the same feeling I felt when Amber told me to think of my mom so that I could find her. It was an intense, deep feeling, more so that when I first tried connecting to her.

"I love you, right up to the moon and back," sounded the woman on the screen.

As the woman on screen finished reading the bedtime story, I could see a change in my mother's eyes. The lines cascading from the corner of her eyes began to glisten. A tear fell and stained the deep grooves down the side of her face.

The mother had closed the book and reached down to hug the young boy in his bed. The silence of the moment was broken by a soft, almost indistinguishable voice. My mother wiped the fallen tear from her cheek. "I love you, Orion."

CHAPTER 11

The next few days were spent studying my mother. I would watch her move from the couch, to the fridge, then back. She would wake up, pour a glass of wine, watch TV then, rinse and repeat for hours on end. She slept and I stood at the foot of her bed, just watching. Her husband played a minor part in her life and would either accompany her on the couch as they stared blankly at the changing scenes and characters or meander through the house, tinkering with some random piece of dusty relic he had found lying around.

I couldn't see any need for me to be a Guardian for the shell of a woman I used to know. I had yet to deal with the full range of emotions that would accompany a bittersweet reunion between my mother and me. I was pretty sure she had no idea I had even died. I had no family other than her—none I had kept in contact with, anyway—and there would therefore be nobody to notify or arrange a funeral. Not to mention the fact there was no body for the general public to bury.

That was until I noticed my mother stare out of the kitchen window one morning during my week of body babysitting.

The sun had barely begun to break through the low morning clouds the distance. The air was becoming cooler, but just a hint of fall could be felt in the air outside. My mother's furnace had started to turn on the last two days, and she was wearing house slippers to protect her feet from the chill of the linoleum throughout the house. I, of course, couldn't feel the chill, but my mother's hunched-over frame seemed to curl in a little tighter as she tried to protect any more heat from escaping her withered body. She poured a cup of whiskey using coffee as a creamer and stood in front of the dirty window.

"Orion," her voice was small, but carried firmly, "wherever you are, whatever you're doing, I'm sorry. I wish I could have told you when you were alive." Her eyes, wet with sadness, were a cool blue. No tears fell, but her voice was deep with despair and pain. Her weathered hands clutched her cup a little tighter.

"Mom? Can you... Can you hear me?"

Silence.

No head-turning to me in acknowledgement.

"Orion, she doesn't know you're here." The soft, melodic voice came from behind me, shaking me out of my trance.

"Shit!" I quickly turned and instinctively reached for a weapon that wasn't holstered to my side. "Amber, you can't do that! I damn near had a heart attack." If I'd had any breath in my lungs, it would have been forced out. Apparently you can't sense other spirits sneaking up on you.

Her smirk was quick and light. "I'd apologize, but then I'd be lying. I never could sneak up on you when we were souls. This is going to be fun." She winked and it hit me deep.

"Amber, I'm going to put a bell around your neck just so I can hear you coming." Checking over my shoulder, I could see my mom had moved from the window and was making her way over to the couch.

"That's some of little things that you'll find out as you work your way through the first few months of being a Guardian. You can't hear other Guardians or spirits. Archs can sense all other spirits. They have a kind of built-in awareness of all supernatural beings. We, however, don't get that. We're not so lucky! I've been told they *feel* the spirits as they come into proximity to them, but we don't make sounds. Michael told me it's like that feeling when you reach out to your assigned soul, but slightly different depending on the nature of the spirit." With her explanation, she reached for my hand and gestured for me to follow. Her hand sliding into mine still felt like the first time, way back after our date at Morty's. That feeling would never grow old.

"So, how is it that I feel you right now, but I can't hear you ambush me?"

"There are some things that still remain as far as feelings go. Most aspects of touch, taste, and a few other things we remember from life are given to us here.

"Now, I want you to come with me. I feel I need to give you a crash course on some things that have changed since you were brought here."

With that, we walked to the door and appeared in a cleared out meadow in a forest that looked vaguely familiar. We were in a valley in the Uintah mountains. Amber and I had been camping here once. The creek in the distance bubbled softly as she faced me. The dense green pines stood guard around us. "I thought this would be as good a place as any to go over a few things."

We both took in the surroundings. The meadow grass bristled slightly in the easy breeze as it trickled through the trees.

"Ry, the souls we are given to watch over can't hear us. They can't see us. We're told not to interact directly with them, but truth be told we have the ability. Michael told you that you aren't supposed to interfere with their surroundings. That still stands true, but there are times when we need to redirect the things around them." As she said the word *redirect*, she made quotations in the air. She explained that we can't alter anything to take them out of their predestined end of fate, but sometimes things happen that aren't in the plans. She had never had this come up with her assigned soul, Louise Jorgensen. Louise was an elderly woman who was a retired elementary teacher. Louise wasn't in direct danger like Lynn was. Amber went on explaining that she knew some of the other Guardians whose souls were targeted—like my mother. They had told her that sometimes Lucifer's demons would try and change the timeline the souls were given in order to hasten their end.

"It's a lot like when you're in the gym and trying to lift a heavy bench press... You dig deep for that extra little bit so you can rack the bar after your last rep. You pull the strength from your core and focus on the object that you're trying to move." As the last words slipped from her lips, she swatted at a nearby branch of pine, knocking a pinecone thirty feet from the limb. "See? Now you try it."

I focused on an opposing branch near the one she had swung at where a fairly large pinecone dangled. I tightened my core and raised my arm, swinging hard at the ball of shingled pine. I tried to knock the pinecone off the branch and hit it over the big green monster in Fenway Park some fifteen-hundred miles away. I missed wildly and fell hard to the rough ground, filling my mouth with dirt and rock. Amber laughed so hard she fell over, holding her stomach. "Attagirl, boy. Try again! This time concentrate on hitting the pinecone instead of trying to kill it. It's not about the force, it's about intent."

I brushed myself off and planted my feet firmly. I closed my eyes and remembered a time during a mission when I had slipped from a rock ledge as my team and I crawled down the face of an outcropping to get to a small cave where insurgents had cached some weapons. I was sucked up against the rock face when my feet slipped. I could feel the empty pit in my stomach explode, anticipating my fall. As my feet flung towards to rock, trying to get a last second footing, I threw my hand up and grabbed a small crag, saving me from plummeting the remaining ten feet to what would have been at least a broken ankle, let alone a compromise to our mission. I had to find that rock, grab it, and hold on to prevent my fall. I wasn't going to compromise the task at hand.

My eyes sprung open and I eagle-eyed the pinecone. With my right arm raised, I swung at the target. As my hand neared the pinecone, I could feel the muscles in my body tense as if I was bracing for a spear tackle from a speeding linebacker. The muscles in my arm tingled as I slapped the pinecone off of the branch, sending it tumbling across the open meadow.

"Just. Like. That. Not too bad, Ry. Could you tell the difference from the first time you tried?"

"Yeah! It was as if I could feel the nerves engage as my arm flew towards it, and then—boom!"

Looking down at my hand, I expected to see a glowing aura around my fingers.

"There isn't any visual change in our bodies, but it is something we feel instead."

I spent the next few minutes knocking every pinecone in reach off their limbs, honing my new skill. By the time that we were done, I'd plucked every accessible hanging target in the surrounding trees.

Amber watched and critiqued my form as I ran from branch to branch, swinging wildly but with clear intent. Once the trees were cleared, she called me to a spot in the middle of the clearing. She sat down on the grass, patting an area directly in front of her. As I sat cross-legged in front of her, I could tell something was weighing on her. Her soft eyes had taken on an almost sorrowful yet serious look.

"Orion, I told you my soul isn't in immediate danger... That's why I reached out to some of the other Guardians whose souls are like your—you know, sought after for whatever reason. There will more than likely come a time when you have to face a demon. Lucifer—Luc, as he is known to us—has an army of them that number in the thousands. They have abilities that we don't, and some we don't understand, and they will use tactics that are dirty to say the least. You need to be aware of some of these and you need to find your strengths in order to fight them.

"When we are christened as Guardians, we are given strengths. It's not like Superman; we can't fly or shoot lasers from our eyes. The powers we have are based on our past life. They are usually abilities we possessed before but an amplified version. For you to stand a chance, you need to find out what they are—what it is you can do—and master those skills."

Her hands reached forward and rested just above my knees. "I know you were always athletic and strong in your life. Maybe that's where you excel. But it could be something else. In order to find out, you need to search within you and feel where your power is based."

With that, Amber closed her eyes. I felt her hands warm against my pant leg. "Whoa, Amber, I can feel that. I thought we couldn't feel hot or cold?"

Her hands stayed firmly against my legs as her eyes crept open. "One of my strengths is amplifying senses. I can help others change their moods. If someone is angry or scared, I can help calm their fears or rage." I was immediately reminded of many times when I had been having nightmares and flashbacks, and her soft, delicate hands touched my skin. In life she had been able to ease my fear or pain. This made sense after she'd explained how our abilities worked.

Closing my eyes, I tried to concentrate. The breeze had grown to a soft, whistling wind that swayed the upper branches of the trees around us. I could still hear the small creek in the distance. The grass underneath me began to tickle slightly as the wind slithered between Amber and myself. I could hear the far-off call of a hawk. That's when I felt the warm streak inside that I had noticed when Amber first placed her hands on me. The heat grew, and soon my arms and legs felt as if they were filled with flickering warmth.

Amber's voice interrupted the soundtrack of the forest. "There. Keep going, Orion. You're feeling it."

My body had filled with a burgeoning fire. Every muscle seemed to twitch in anticipation. Just then, a small mouse peeked its head from a burrow near our legs. There was no conscious thought to reach for the rodent, but I had struck my hand to the burrow and now held the mouse in my right hand. With my eyes still closed, I held the mouse firmly and raised it in front of Amber. The mouse craned its head back and forth as it wrestled against my grip. I opened my eyes and looked at my catch. I wasn't squeezing enough to hurt it, but it wasn't going anywhere any time soon.

"Would you look at that? If we were able to eat, it doesn't look like we would go hungry."

I assessed what had just happened. I was able to not only physically grab the nimble mouse, but I had snatched it from beside me and now raised it up like a trophy, high into the air. I let the snared mouse loose on the ground as he scampered quickly back to the safety of his hole in the mountain dirt.

"It looks like you've got the physical abilities thing down and you just might have some speed and alertness thrown in for good measure, too. Not too shabby for a rookie Guardian."

"My eyes were closed the entire time, but it was like I could still *see* him, right beside me. I was always able to tell if someone was trying to sneak up on me, and it came in rather handy a time or three on our missions."

"You'll find out that these things come easier with time and practice. For now, however, I need to check in on Louise, so let's get you back." Amber stood and brushed off the little bit of earth from her legs.

"Amber, you seemed to be able to find me rather easy. How do I know where *you* are? In case I need to, you know, ask you a question or just see that radiant smile?" Our hands met like magnets as we began walking towards the tree line.

"Ry, all you need to do, in order to find me or any other Guardian, is to think of them. Think with your heart. Reach out to me with an imaginary tether and, if you do it right, you'll travel to me."

"Like an air Uber? Nice." I could never get tired of hearing her soft laugh, even if it were somewhat forced at my idiotic jokes.

"Yeah, just like that, ya goof."

The trees disappeared and we were right back at the house where my mom and Floyd wasted the days away.

Nothing had changed. They both sat on the couch while a rerun of The Andy Griffith show played, mostly unwatched. The empty wine glass sat in my mother's hand, beckoning to the collapsed box in the kitchen. Floyd was slumped over slightly, softly snoring. I turned to look at Amber, ready to make a sarcastic comment about the high profile of my job that was watching an elderly couple breathe, but she was gone.

Hours had passed because the sky outside had begun to turn to dusk. There was no chance of anything else happening at the Sutton household that would require my services, or so I thought.

CHAPTER 12

(Psychiclibrary.com/archangels-for-healing) News of Raphael's death had spread through Celestia like a California wildfire. All of the Guardians were informed immediately. An Arch had never been killed before. Very little was known about how exactly Lucifer had eliminated him, but there was no doubt that a huge void had been drawn in the ranks of Heaven. The Creator had met with the remaining Archangels in order to enforce the dire situation at hand. Raphael had been the Archangel of healing. His loss would have an immediate and compounding impact on the Heavens, not to mention over the souls of Earth. The remaining Archs—Michael, Gabriel, Uriel, Zadkiel, Chamuel, and Ariel—now had to shoulder the duties of their fallen brother.

Michael is the leader of the Archangels, their commanding general. He is Father's right-hand Archangel. People often seek Michael's help with protection, especially members of the military and police. He has been employed in every single war that the Souls of Earth has ever fought. Some of these wars were on a large scale, like the infamous World Wars I and II. Some wars lasted less than an hour. One such war was the Anglo-Zanzibar War, fought on August 27, 1896. Regardless of the size of the fight, Michael has been there, watching over both sides. There were no sides to favor. There has always been right and wrong, but war was a creation of man. Of course, Lucifer had his influence and employed his demons to do his bidding, but Father favored no side.

Gabriel was the second in command within the ranks of the Archangels. Gabriel was the one to oversee communication. He also helps with strength and communication between Souls. Sometimes, Souls have an extended ability to sense things outside of the human realm, and the veil between Celestia and them is a little thinner. That's where Gabriel comes in. Not everyone is given these abilities; they are chosen based on needs, strengths, and their heart. Much like Michael, Gabriel was a physical specimen to be beheld. Standing at just over six feet, Gabriel had a presence that was immediately noticed. However, unlike Michael, Gabriel was not as formidable when he spoke. Gabriel's voice had an instant effect whenever he spoke. The room and any surrounding noises all but instantly fell silent. All anyone ever heard when Gabriel spoke was Gabriel himself. The smooth, baritone sound made it clear he was the one proficient in communication. Gabriel's hair is long curly locks of surfer blonde that fall on his shoulders.

Uriel is the Archangel to whom Souls turn when they seek wisdom and knowledge. When someone seeks to know the truth or is looking for guidance in any given situation, they call upon him. Uriel also helps protect couples from destruction and helps to grow the love that is found between them. Uriel's build was thin, but not small by any means. He looked much like a cowboy. His muscles, like ropes, were tight; as if he had ridden bulls for fun after hours of farming. And where Gabriel's curly locks of surfer blonde fell down to his shoulders, Uriel's brown hair gave hints of red whenever the light hit it just right.

Zadkiel is the Archangel of mercy. When Souls are wronged by another, whether a stranger, a friend, a lover, or a family member, Zadkiel oversees the solution and helps resolve the pain by helping whomever was wronged to find forgiveness. Human bodies require physical medicine and healing when they are hurt, and much is the same with human minds; they, too, require healing. Zadkiel also watches over the development of Souls in a spiritual sense.

Chamuel is the Archangel over peace, love, and relationships. He embodies compassion and love and helps to develop that in the Souls of Earth. This is also applicable to self-love. Often Souls can easily love others, but have a much harder time finding love for themselves. Chamuel assists by helping the Soul find inner peace. Once that inner peace is established, love can flourish.

Ariel watches over the animals and all living things of the Earth. Ariel watches over all elemental aspects of Earth, too. Ariel is an ancient and wise Archangel who some have forever called "Mother Earth". Ariel isn't particularly fond of this moniker. In fact, it's a slight at Father's partner, Mother.

CHAPTER 13

The sky outside grew dark much faster than the typical fall evening would; that's when I saw the impending storm rolling in on the distant horizon. The twinkling of lights showed a dance of lightning within the clouds. Turning to look at the withered pair on the couch, I was reminded that they were oblivious to everything around them, even the TV that stared back at them.

I stood up from the tattered chair facing the slumped pair and walked to the window. That's when I felt the pain.

It was a pinpoint, searing pain focused directly in the middle of my chest. What I thought was a red hot ice pick burying itself into my torso was invisible. My mind tried to assess what was happening. If I was dead, could I have a heart attack? Of course not. *Don't be stupid, Orion.* Yet there it was, slowly growing to what now measured to the size of a baseball. The tormenting heat spread from the center of my chest and was now felt through my whole upper body.

"What the hell?" I looked to my mom and Floyd, but of course they couldn't hear me. They were oblivious to the fact I stood in their dilapidated house. Fear began to seep into my thoughts as I raced to figure out what was happening. I began to pull at the shirt I wore—and that's when the flash lit up the yard out front.

In a split-second, the pain exploded inside me and disappeared even quicker. The illuminated explosion out front tore my eyes from my clothes and chest to the tree that stood guard by the sidewalk. It was there I saw the taunting yellow eyes looking directly at me. There was no body, only eyes. A small, dull shimmer of white grew just below the eyes until an evil smirk lay just below the evil, yellow glowing eyes.

The pain filling my chest was replaced with a different kind of fire. I could feel a boiling surge soon filling every limb. I walked to the front door, pushing through to the outside. The light rain sprinkled the ground as the wind blew it every which way. By now the eyes and sneer had grown a head. It looked like the head of a Pitbull as the body began to fill the distance between it and the ground. When it had finished appearing, I was facing what looked to be the mutated offspring of a manged dog and a hulking, disfigured gorilla. The creature had muscles—much like that of a human—, but the skin was dark black and covered with coarse, black hair. The head resembled a square-shaped canine form.

The distant lightning brought with it a low grumbling thunder, or so I thought; I soon realized the growling was coming from the figure fifteen feet in front of me.

The wind and rain falling on the houses around us were soon non-existent as the creature gargled the threat from deep in his throat. "You're useless, Orion. You've only just begun and are nothing more than fresh meat. There's nothing you can do to stop me from taking her."

The old familiar thrill of a fight incinerated my insides. The burning had risen and encompassed all that I was. I didn't recognize the voice that shot words into the dark night, but it came from somewhere deep inside me. "Hell hath no fury like a soldier prepared to fight. I can promise you two things will happen tonight: One, you're not going to lay"—looking for hands on the creature I saw nothing more than mangled, claw-like paws— "whatever the hell you have for chicken chokers on anyone, especially that woman inside; and two, when this is all said and done, I'll have eaten your fucking soul." Michael and all of Celestia would have to learn that you can't have a lethal fighting force without a few additional adjectives.

The creature crouched and readied for a lunging attack, just as the sky filled with a bright, white lightning bolt. As the light flashed, he leapt with precision in my direction. I felt the mountain of tense, muscular hate crash into me, knocking me back, sending us tumbling. This thing was obviously a demon and could pack one hell of a punch. When we stopped rolling, I was pinned to the ground by the creature's dog-like legs as he hailed fists into my face.

Every hit felt like a truck being slammed into me. Through the barrage of painful blows, I tried to think what Amber had taught me not more than a couple hours before. I could feel the weight of the demon on me, but I couldn't budge. My legs thrashed upward as I tried to knee the beast's back, but I failed miserably. Through the pounding I closed my eyes for a brief second, and then it started; the boiling of force inside me came through in one focused movement as the demon flew back through the air. He was thrown back ten feet as my arms shot from under his legs and threw him off of me. I was standing over the beast in a swift move that now saw my foot planted directly on his chest. The glaring, hate-filled eyes of the hellish gorilla dog were now filled with nothing but fear. This was going to be fun.

Every time my fist balled and impaled the demon's snarled face, he shrieked in pain. The hits landed with such force that, each time I struck him, the ground shook. After peppering the demon with jabs and blows, my hand curled around its throat. Raising and holding the feral creature a foot off the ground, I looked up into its now-wide yellow eyes. "I want you to give a message to whomever it is that runs the kennel you escaped from. Tell him if anyone or anything"—I looked the beast up and down for effect—"sets foot or paw near that woman again, I will end them." With the last words having been said, I crushed the throat of the demon. His body fell limp and dangled from my hand, still raised before me. The eyes, once piercing and yellow, were now an empty, dull gray.

I dropped the carcass to the wet ground below and watched as the body turned to smoke and dissipate into the night. My body, still shaking from the fight, stood stoic above the cold, bare ground. The drumming rain was interrupted by Amber's voice immediately behind me.

"Orion, are you okay?" Her hand rested sympathetically upon my back as I turned to face her. Her face wore a mask of concern as she inspected me for injuries. "You're not hurt?" Her words, laced with surprise, trickled into the air.

"I don't think so. I don't feel anything." I said as I patted myself to double-check. That's when I jerked my head to look at the house. "My mom!"

"She's fine, Ry. I just checked. They're both asleep."

We walked to the house. As we entered the living room, they were just where Amber had said they were, doing exactly what they were doing before the night's episode took a turn. My mind hadn't registered everything that had just happened, but one thing stood out to me. "Amber, tonight, before I saw the demon, I *felt* him." Placing my hand over where my heart should be, I emphasized my last words. "I. *Felt*. Him. Before I even knew he was there, I felt a pain in my chest. It was a hot, searing pain, right here." Again, I patted my chest. "You told me. You said that only Archs can sense them. Amber, I knew he was there. I turned around and he was standing right there." Pointing to the spot outside, in the storm, where the demon had begun taunting me.

"Orion, that's... that's not possible. I mean, the only way that could happen was if..." Her voice trailed off as she stared right into my eyes, reminding me of every single second we had spent together when we were alive. Her hands, once calmingly draped on my arms, now fell slowly to her sides. She wore disbelief like an old, weathered mask. Her mouth parted and we stood, staring in at each other, as the impossible thought we shared lingered in the air.

"If what you're saying happened—and I mean *actually happened*, Ry—you would have to be an Archangel. You would have to be one of the *Chosen* ones in order to have escalated abilities." Her eyes glazed in disbelief as she tried to keep her poker face intact.

"Yeah, I think I get that, babe, but I swear... It happened. I was standing right here." I motioned to the very spot where we were standing. "I was looking out the window at the storm clouds. That's when I felt the pain in my chest. It hurt worse than anything I've ever felt and then, when I turned around, I saw the demon's eyes. In the dark. By the tree. When I started walking outside, the feeling kept growing until my whole body filled with a kind of electric surging. I felt like I could rock this house off its foundation. I felt raw power inside of me. Before I knew it, the demon, the beast—whatever it was—, was on top of me and beating me like I owed it money. I couldn't move and I couldn't hit it. I focused through the flailing punches, and the next thing I knew I had thrown him over by the tree. I picked him up and crushed his throat like it was a plastic straw. He had to have been a couple hundred pounds, but I had him held up, stealing the air from him like he weighed nothing." My animation ended as I stopped talking with my hands and looked down to meet Amber's eyes.

"Orion, we need to go see Michael. Now." She reached for my hand as I jerked it back.

"I can't go anywhere," I protested. "Not after that thing just tried to kill her!"

"Orion, she'll be fine. Lucifer won't send another demon so soon after that one. Not after what you did to it. I'm sure he's just as surprised as we are. He's going to be rethinking his plan of attack before trying anything. Besides, I've called out to some of the other Guardians in the area. They are going to watch over her. It's broadcast through Celestia when a demon attacks. Everybody knows right now what happened. Your mom, not to mention all of Earth, is safe right now."

My hand in hers, we shifted to the Great Hall.

The large hall looked the same as the first time I'd been there, except there were candles adorning the walls. Their flickering lights glowed warmly against the hundreds of thousands of books and shelves. We stood in the center of the Hall, near the large, round table where the Book sat. I looked forward again to see Michael was gauging me with a sly smile on his face.

"What was it you said? You were going to *eat his effing soul*?" A small chuckle bled through his lips as he began again. "Orion, you did great. It looks like Amber has shown you some of the tricks of the trade?" Michael made his statement and waited patiently for an answer.

"Michael, was that thing a demon? I mean, it was one ugly moth—"

"Ah, ah, ah. Yes, it was a demon. Luc has a sick, twisted sense of humor when it comes to creating demons. He likes to cross breed species and slap them together. He thinks it will instill fear in the Guardians they are sent to face." His words cut me off and were a subtle reminder to me about the language rule in Celestia.

"Okay, so a demon tried to take me out in order to kill my mom, but there's one thing about what happened that I don't understand..." I was still in disbelief, and I'm sure it showed on my face.

Michael straightened himself and slowly took in a breath as if making a formal announcement. "Orion, you're forthcoming question is a valid one, and one that deserves an answer, but you already know what that answer is. We've all been watching you. Amber has given you a few bits and pieces of training in order to help prepare you for your work as a Guardian. What she didn't know was why, exactly, Father called you up sooner than He had anticipated." Michael turned as he spoke and began walking down one of the long hallways that met the rotunda of the Great Hall. Amber and I took that as our invitation to follow him.

Michael continued, "Father, I think, had an idea that something was about to happen and sent us to recruit you. We were told to make it happen at any and all costs. 'Make him understand', He told us. Orion, I always knew you were destined to be here with us as a Guardian. The thing is, Father didn't recruit you to be a Guardian. You were recruited to be an *Archangel*." Stopping to look me in the eyes and drive home the last sentence, Michael now continued walking down the hallway, which was lined with doors leading to numerous unknown rooms.

"Orion, there is one thing you should know. Archangels are the elite Guardians of Celestia. We are the ones who look over all souls of Earth. In rare cases, Father assigns us to specific souls in order to protect them. You will continue to watch over Lynn Sutton and ensure nothing like what happened the other night happens again. You must protect her at all costs."

CHAPTER 14

As we walked the marble hallway within the Great Hall, I noticed that our steps never echoed. There was no sound. The floor was an ocean of square, white marble pieces. The walls were stacked with doors for the first hundred feet or so and then opened up into another large open space that looked like the foyer of an elegant theater. The walls rose high above and fell into archways that carved themselves high into the ceiling. There was a wall that was made entirely of glass. The glass wasn't exactly clear or see-through. It appeared more blue-ish and gave way to a faint scene outside. The wall to our right turned a corner and led to a set of dark, wooden doors that arched high above, meeting the ceiling and matching the archways that lined the hallway to our left.

Michael motioned for us to follow him through the doors. The room was dark except for a faint, soft white glow near a dimly lit wall. The room itself was rather small, but the feeling when we walked inside was larger than the Great Hall. By the time that I had fully stepped inside the room, I was overtaken with powerful emotions. I was elated and felt absolute, unequivocal, and pure love. It was a mother's love, but stronger than one person could handle. It was happiness, but registered far beyond any happiness that I had ever felt before. Underneath it all was an old, familiar feeling. One that had dominated years ago on the hard dirt of every foreign country that I had set foot on. A feeling that overwhelmingly fulfilled me because I knew it was my calling.

As I took another step inside the room, I could see just what the light came from. The glowing adornment hung on the wall in a beautiful display. The grand spread of white, feathered wings hung across the entire width of the wall. The wings were spread as if in flight. There were no strings or hooks that I could see keeping them afloat. The tips sharply ended and were 12 feet across from each other. The center of the wings were separated by a small space between two bundles of white. The inner pieces looked as if they, too, were made of feathers. Michael, facing me, said three words. The words were simple enough, but I immediately felt the weight of them as they left his lips. "Are you ready?" His eyes, still soft in look, held piercing gazes and I could sense the seriousness of what he was implying.

"Yes, sir." The words felt firm and sure as I said them. I had unintentionally stood taller and my body assumed the position of attention without me trying to do so. Michael placed his hand on my shoulder and guided me to the spot in the center of the wall where the wings met at the two bundles. He motioned towards the floor for me to kneel and as I did, I was overcome with a powerful, strength. It was as if my entire body was a raging river flowing with adrenaline. Electric and violent power caged only by skin. As I knelt down on one knee my head bowed as I assumed a position much like that of someone who was to be knighted. When my head bowed, my eyes closed, and the room exploded with warm light. I could see through my eyelids the flash of brilliance that filled the small room. Before I could register what had caused the light, it was over. That's when I felt the weight. The strength I had felt surging through me had attached to my broad back in the form of wings.

I was now, officially, an Archangel of Heaven.